FALKIRK COMMUNITY TRUST

30124 02685331 9

KU-239-424

Falkirk
Community
Trust

FALKIRK COMMUNITY
TRUST LIBRARIES

THE GREEK'S
FORBIDDEN
INNOCENT

THE GREEK'S FORBIDDEN INNOCENT

ANNIE WEST

MILLS & BOON

All rights reserved including the right of reproduction
in whole or in part in any form. This edition is
published by arrangement with Harlequin Books S.A.

This is a work of fiction. Names, characters,
places, locations and incidents are purely fictional
and bear no relationship to any real life individuals,
living or dead, or to any actual places, business
establishments, locations, events or incidents.
Any resemblance is entirely coincidental.

This book is sold subject to the condition that it
shall not, by way of trade or otherwise, be lent, resold,
hired out or otherwise circulated without the prior consent
of the publisher in any form of binding or cover
other than that in which it is published and without a
similar condition including this condition being
imposed on the subsequent purchaser.

® and TM are trademarks owned and used by the
trademark owner and/or its licensee. Trademarks
marked with ® are registered with the United Kingdom
Patent Office and/or the Office for Harmonisation in the
Internal Market and in other countries.

First published in Great Britain 2019
by Mills & Boon, an imprint of HarperCollins*Publishers*
1 London Bridge Street, London, SE1 9GF

Large Print edition 2019

© 2019 Annie West

ISBN: 978-0-263-08243-2

FALKIRK COUNCIL LIBRARIES

MIX
Paper from
responsible sources
FSC® C007454

This book is produced from independently certified
FSC™ paper to ensure responsible forest management. For
more information visit www.harpercollins.co.uk/green.

Printed and bound in Great Britain
by CPI Group (UK) Ltd, Croydon, CR0 4YY

This story is for Helen Sibbritt.

Thank you so much
for your enthusiasm, support
and never-failing good cheer!

CHAPTER ONE

'TAKE A DEEP BREATH, Carissa, and tell me slowly.' Mina held her friend's shoulders tight. 'And another.' She nodded encouragingly as Carissa's breathing grew more normal. 'That's better.'

While Carissa focused on her breathing, Mina's gaze searched for the source of her friend's distress. But there was nothing unusual in the entry to the other woman's apartment. No blood. No disarray. No intruder. Just a large pink suitcase.

Yet something was definitely wrong. Carissa, the most easygoing person she knew, had grabbed Mina before she could open the door to her own apartment and yanked her in next door. There was real fear in Carissa's china-blue eyes.

'Come and sit and tell me about it.'

'No!' Carissa shook her head and a cloud of golden curls spilled around her shoulders. 'There's no time. They'll be here soon. *But I don't want to go. I can't go.*' Tears filled her eyes as her voice wobbled. 'I want Pierre! But he's not here in Paris. He's abroad.'

That at least made sense. Pierre was Carissa's boyfriend.

'Don't fret. No one's going to make you go anywhere you don't want to.' Mina kept her voice calm, ushering her friend into the small sitting room and gently pushing her into a seat. Carissa's whole body shook and her face was stark white.

Mina had received enough bad news herself to recognise shock. Her mother had died when she was young and just five years ago, when she was seventeen, her father had died unexpectedly from a brain aneurism.

Memories stirred of that terrifying time, held hostage in a palace coup after her father's funeral. Then her sister Ghizlan's sacrifice, forced to wed the coup leader, Huseyn, so he could become Sheikh. It seemed a lifetime away from Mina's life now in France.

'Tell me what's up so I can help.' Mina pulled a chair close and took Carissa's hands. Her face was, for the first time Mina could recall, bare of make-up and her shirt wasn't buttoned right. For

Carissa this was a fashion catastrophe. More like Mina's usual look than her own.

Mina's frown deepened. 'Has someone hurt you?'

Her stomach clenched as she remembered the day of the coup, the drench of icy fear as a soldier manhandled her, stopping her escape with brutal efficiency. She recalled the adrenalin rush galvanising her to fight back. It was the first time anyone had laid a hand on her. The first time she'd become aware of the sheer, physical power men could exert over women. Until then, Mina's royal status had protected her.

Carissa was trusting and gentle, always looking for the best in people. If someone had taken advantage of her—

'No, it's nothing like that.'

Mina's shoulders sagged. Relief rushed through her. In the years they'd studied together at a prestigious Paris art school, and since, she'd never seen Carissa distraught like this.

'So who is coming? Where don't you want to go?'

Carissa's bottom lip quivered and she blinked hard.

'Alexei Katsaros is sending someone. They'll

take me to his private island.' A shudder ran through her. 'But I don't want to go. I can't. Even when Dad told me about it, I never thought it would actually *happen*! You have to help me, Mina. Please.'

Mina's worry eased and with it her frantic heartbeat. Not a life-and-death situation, then. She knew who Alexei Katsaros was. Who didn't? He was a megawealthy IT entrepreneur. Carissa's father was one of his executives.

'Is it an invitation to visit your father? I'm sure Pierre would spare you for a short vacation.'

Carissa shook her head. 'This isn't a vacation. It's an arranged marriage! Dad told me he hoped to organise it but I never thought he'd bring it off. Alexei Katsaros can have his pick of women.'

Mina said nothing. Carissa was extraordinarily pretty and sweet-natured. That, plus her innate desire to please, would appeal to lots of men.

'I can't go through with it, Mina.' Carissa's fingers bit into hers. 'I could never love a man like that, so hard and judgemental. He wants a trophy wife, who'll do what he wants when he wants. My father's told him I'm pretty and bid-dable and...' Her shoulders shook as the tears became sobs. 'I never thought it would come to this. It seemed impossible, laughable. But I don't have a choice. My father's *counting* on me.'

Mina frowned. Arranged marriages she knew about. If her father had lived he'd have organised one for her.

'I'm sure no one will force you into anything.' Unlike in Jeirut. Her sister had been forced into an unwanted marriage and Mina remembered feeling utterly helpless at being unable to prevent it. It had been a miracle when, against the odds, the pair later fell in love. The match had seemed doomed to end in misery. 'Your father will be there. If you explain—'

'But he's *not* there,' Carissa wailed. 'I don't know where he is. I can't contact him. And I can't say no to Mr Katsaros. Dad warned me there'd been some trouble at work. He didn't say what, but I think his job's on the line. He's hoping this marriage will smooth everything over.' Carissa clung to Mina's hands, her fingers curling into talons. 'But I could never marry such a hard man. He has a new woman every week. Besides, Pierre and I are in love. We're getting married.' A flicker of happiness transformed her teary features.

'You're getting married?' Mina stared. She shouldn't be surprised; the pair were besotted.

Carissa's smile died. 'We were planning to elope next weekend, when he's back from this business trip. Pierre says it will be easier to face his family with a fait accompli.'

Pierre rose in Mina's estimation. He was a lovely guy but he'd never stood up to his stiff-necked family who wanted him to marry some-one from old French money.

'But I can't marry him if I'm forced to marry Alexei Katsaros!' Carissa's tears overflowed.

'Did Katsaros *say* he wanted to marry you?'

'As good as. He said my father had told him about me and he was anxious to meet. He be-lieved we'd find a lot in common and that we had a future together.' Carissa bit her lip. 'I tried to fob him off but he didn't hear a word I said. He cut me off and said his staff would be here in an hour to collect me. What will I do?'

Mina frowned. She didn't like the sound of this. He might be rich but that didn't excuse rudeness or give him the right to order Carissa around.

'Tell me again exactly what your father told you.'

But as Carissa spoke, Mina's hope that her friend had overreacted dissolved. There'd re-cently been a rift between her father and his em-ployer. After years of faithful service it seemed

Katsaros might dump him. Mina couldn't approve of Mr Carter's plan to use Carissa to cement his position, but such things happened. Several of Mina's peers in Jeirut had been married to older men they barely knew to strengthen family or business links.

She gritted her teeth, watching Carissa's hands flutter as she related the one-sided conversation with Alexei Katsaros. He hadn't invited Carissa to his island hideaway but simply informed her of the travel arrangements. As if she were freight to be transported, not a woman with a life of her own.

Mina's temper rose like steam from a kettle.

She prized her freedom, appreciating how different her life was in Paris, away from a world where every major decision was made by the male head of her family. Western women accepted freedom as their right, not knowing how precious that was. And here was some billionaire bully, trying to snatch that from Carissa. With the help of her own father!

It wasn't right.

'And there's nothing I can do.' Carissa sniffled.

'Of course there is. They can't force you onto the plane. Or into marriage.'

'I can't not go. What about my father's job?'

She hiccupped. 'But if I go, what about Pierre? His family will find a way to stop our wedding.'

Mina wanted to tell Carissa to grow a backbone and stand up for herself. But Carissa wasn't made that way. Besides, she cared for her father, though he'd got her into this mess. Plus it sounded, from other things she'd said, as if Mr Carter hadn't recovered from his wife's recent death. That might explain why he'd slipped up at work. A good employer would make allowances for grief. Mina suspected Alexei Katsaros was a domineering tyrant, considering no one but himself.

Irresistibly, her thoughts dragged back to those fraught days after her father's death. Her future and her sister's had hung in the balance, their fate determined by a man with little sympathy for their hopes and wishes.

Mina remembered the horror of being utterly powerless.

She refused to let Carissa become a chattel to buy her father out of trouble, or satisfy Katsaros's desire for a convenient, biddable wife.

'I've packed a bag. I can't reach my father, so I'll have to go. But it means leaving Pierre.' Carissa wrung her hands and Mina felt something snap inside.

Carissa was sweet but she had as much grit

as a marshmallow. Between them, Katsaros and Carter could herd her into a marriage that would make her miserable for the rest of her life. Mina couldn't change her friend into a woman who'd look a thug in the eye and send him packing, or tell her father he couldn't marry her off to a stranger. But she *could* delay things long enough for Carissa and Pierre to marry. A few days, a week at most.

'How long before they collect you?'

Carissa's answer was drowned by a sharp rap on the door. She gasped and grabbed Mina's hands.

The last shred of doubt fled Mina's brain as she read her friend's terror and despair. Carissa was a pushover, but Mina wasn't.

She got to her feet.

'Still no sign of Carter, sir. He hasn't been home.'

Alexei's grip tightened on the phone and he ground his teeth in frustration. But he refrained from chewing out the head of his London office. It wasn't MacIntyre's fault Carter had done a bunk. Alexei should have acted sooner, but initially he hadn't wanted to believe Carter's guilt. The man had been at his side for years, the only person Alexei really trusted.

That was why his betrayal cut so deep. Trust came hard to Alexei. He'd seen his mother betrayed and cast aside, made into a victim and her life shortened, because she trusted too easily.

Alexei bore a lot of the blame. He'd been gullible, falling for his stepfather's charm, believing the man genuinely cared. He'd persuaded his mother to let the guy into their lives. Too late they discovered he'd only cultivated Alexei to get to his mother and her dead husband's insurance payment.

No one could accuse Alexei of gullibility now.

That was what made it so remarkable that, despite his caution, he'd come to believe in Carter. It wasn't just his way with numbers. His almost uncanny knack for identifying problems and possible solutions. It was his reticence, his scrupulous separation of business and personal life. He'd been the perfect executive.

Until his double-dealing came to light.

Alexei felt that sucker punch of betrayal. Worse this time because he should have known better. He was no innocent kid.

'Keep me informed. Have the investigator check in daily.'

'Yes, sir. Of course, sir.'

Alexei ended the call and scraped a hand

through his hair, telling himself he'd grown soft. He should have acted sooner. Now he had to play catch-up.

He swung round to pace, ignoring the turquoise water and white sand beyond the window. He didn't want to be in the Caribbean, no matter how restful his private retreat. He wanted to be wherever Carter was. The man's depredations had been deep. Not enough to destabilise Alexei's business but enough to send a ripple of disquiet through anyone savvy enough to discover Alexei had been duped.

Despite his policy of employing the best, most innovative people in the industry, Alexei Katsaros *was* his company as far as the market was concerned. He'd worked hard to establish one of the world's leading software companies and build a reputation as a canny entrepreneur. His nose for success was only rivalled by his company's groundbreaking IT solutions. News of his fallibility would crack that image and damage his company's position.

Damn Carter. Where was he hiding?

Alexei slammed to a halt as he heard a vehicle through the open window.

At last. The ace up his sleeve.

Alexei breathed deep, easing cramped lungs,

assuring himself that now, *finally*, he had the upper hand.

He crossed to the window and watched as the four-wheel drive pulled up. The driver's door opened but before Henri could get out the front passenger door swung open and someone alighted.

Alexei's brow twitched into a frown. That couldn't be her. He waited for the rear door to open but it stayed steadfastly shut. Henri walked ponderously to the rear of the vehicle and pulled out a single suitcase of candy pink.

That was all. One suitcase and one passenger, though not the passenger he expected.

Alexei's frown became a scowl. The call from Paris had assured him that she'd been collected from her apartment and deposited on his jet. Yet surely this wasn't Carter's daughter. He'd expected a fashion tragic with mountains of luggage.

His gaze rested on the svelte figure of a woman who stood, hands on her hips and head back, surveying his home. Far from being addicted to high-end fashion as he'd been led to believe, she wasn't dressed in designer casuals for a tropical island holiday, but for...what? A yoga class? An artist's garret?

Understanding took root. *That* was it.

Carter, when he'd raised the preposterous idea of a match between Alexei and his daughter, had waxed voluble about the girl he'd never mentioned in years of employment. He'd wittered on about her beauty and charm, her sweet disposition and eagerness to please. And her aspirations to be an artist in between shopping. She lived in Paris, playing at an artistic career, no doubt funded by the money Carter had embezzled from Alexei.

Pain radiated from Alexei's jaw down his neck to his tight shoulders.

He yanked his thoughts from Carter's crimes to the man's daughter.

She took her pretensions seriously. Or perhaps the outfit was for his benefit, though surely it wasn't designed to please a man. Flat black shoes, black leggings and an oversized black T-shirt that gaped over one shoulder.

Definitely not Alexei's style. He preferred a woman who dressed like a woman.

Yet even as he dismissed Carissa Carter as not his type, his gaze lingered on the length of shapely legs silhouetted in black. Long legs, the sort of legs he'd enjoy wrapped around his waist during sex.

His gaze flicked higher, skimming her slight figure. He supposed, in the right gear, she'd be a perfect clothes horse, but personally he preferred a woman whose curves were more abundant.

Then the tilt of her head altered and he found himself face-to-face with her.

She was too far away for him to make out her features properly. Just good bone structure and dark hair pulled ruthlessly back into a bun. He had the impression of a wide, mobile mouth, but he wasn't paying attention. His thoughts were on the sudden throb pulsing through his belly.

It couldn't be attraction. Not for the daughter of a criminal. A woman whose lifestyle had probably fed her father's depredations. He had no proof Carissa Carter knew of her father's crimes, but she'd benefited. Maybe she'd been in on the scheme, eager to fund her easy life in Paris. Alexei couldn't trust her. He'd play the part of eager suitor, pretending he was in the market for a wife.

As if he needed a third party to find him a woman!

He stared back at her, expecting her to duck her head and pretend not to see him.

Instead she stood motionless, watching as if *he* were under the microscope. It was a curious feeling. Alexei was used to people inclining their heads in agreement or deference. Except women, who tended to stare.

Carissa's bold regard was something altogether different. It sent heat skittering down his spine, drawing every sense to hyperalert.

Finally, after she'd looked her fill, she turned to Henri. Alexei caught a flash of white teeth as she smiled but it was the coltish grace of her movements that held his attention. There was a fluidity to her supple body that reminded him of a Russian ballet dancer with whom he'd once shared a fiery affair. Alexei recalled not only the dancer's grace but her athleticism and body awareness that had taken sexual pleasure to a new level.

He watched Carissa Carter saunter towards his house. Shoulders back, head up, yet she didn't march. Instead that loose-limbed stroll was a symphony of sensual femininity.

For his benefit?

Of course.

His guest might play at being the bohemian artist, but if she was her father's daughter, she'd have her eye on the main game, getting Alexei's money.

For the first time since he'd learned of Carter's betrayal, Alexei smiled.

He didn't want the woman here, except as bait

to draw her father. The fact she'd accepted his summons told him she'd sell herself into marriage with a man she didn't even know. Though she knew the size of his bank balance. That regularly featured in rich lists around the world.

It could be amusing watching her try to seduce him.

CHAPTER TWO

MINA KNEW ABOUT WEALTH. She'd been born royal. But her family riches and privilege were tied to duty, responsibility and service. The palace where she'd grown up had been the nerve centre for her country's administration.

This was pure sybaritic indulgence.

As if it wasn't enough to own a tropical island rimmed with beaches so white they looked like sugar frosting, Alexei Katsaros's home was the last word in luxury. The pool wrapped around the house so every room looked out on water. There was a bar actually in the pool too, so he and his guests wouldn't have to stir from the water to get a drink.

Four-poster daybeds were scattered around the pool, their gauzy hangings romantic and alluring. Her artist's eye appreciated the cushions in turquoise, teal and jade that reflected the vibrant shades of the tropical garden and the sea beyond. Then there were the sculptures in pale stone, which she glimpsed through the greenery. She itched to detour and investigate.

Forcibly she yanked her attention back to the house. The huge entry door stood open. Beside her, Henri waited for her to precede him.

Strange, this momentary hesitation.

All the way from Paris she'd been buoyed by indignation on Carissa's behalf. Now though, Mina knew an uncharacteristic moment of doubt. A wariness at odds with her practice of facing problems head-on.

Her impulsiveness, her father would have said.

Why? Mina wasn't overawed by Katsaros's wealth, or cowed by any threat he could make.

Yet for a moment, as her gaze locked on the big man watching her from inside, something unfamiliar quivered through her. Something starkly unsettling.

An inner voice urged her to flee while she had the chance.

Of course she lifted her chin and stared right back instead.

The bright bowl of azure sky above her seemed to drop lower, the air thickening as she drew a slow, steadying breath. Still, he held her gaze.

Her bloodstream fizzed, making her fingers and the soles of her feet tingle. For a second she wondered if she'd been hit by a bolt of lightning out of the clear sky, till reason told her that was impossible.

Deliberately she turned away, feigning interest in her surroundings. Yet the image imprinted on her retinas wasn't the white mansion with its picture windows, but the powerfully built man whose eyes locked on her. Everything about him, from his wide-set stance to that deep, muscled chest revealed by his open shirt, screamed strength.

Well, Mina was strong too. No bossy tycoon would intimidate her.

Nodding to Henri, she headed for the door.

She was greeted by Henri's wife, Marie, whose smiling eyes and lilting accent made Mina relax in spite of herself.

'Alexei is eager to meet you but perhaps you'd like to freshen up first?'

Mina smiled and shook her head. The flight by private jet had been far from onerous. 'Thank you, but no. I'm eager to meet my host.'

'How…charming.' The deep voice came from beyond Marie. Its cadence drew Mina's skin tight, as if someone dragged a length of rich velvet across it. A shimmer of heat flared low in her body and she had to work to keep her expression bland.

Slowly, so slowly she seemed to feel each muscle and joint move, she turned her head towards the shadows.

Never had Mina been more grateful for her royal upbringing. She'd spent seventeen years learning to look composed and calm, even if she'd never quite mastered regal. At twelve she'd sat on podiums listening to interminable speeches. At fifteen she'd held her own at royal dinners. Her polite interest expression could fool everyone but her sister.

Which meant the man watching her through narrowed eyes had no idea she felt as if someone had sliced the tendons at the backs of her legs.

Mina's knees shook for the merest instant before she stiffened them, but her cool smile remained steady. As for the sizzle in her blood, no one else knew about that.

She waited for him to frown and say she wasn't Carissa Carter. Yet he simply stared down at her from his superior height. Could it really be that he didn't know what Carissa looked like? That flaw in her plan had kept her awake on the flight from Europe. Yet, against the odds, it appeared he didn't. So sure of himself. Arrogant enough to expect everyone to obey his every whim. So unquestioning.

Mina let her mouth curve slightly. 'Mr Katsaros. How lovely to meet you at last.'

'At *last*, Ms Carter? You've been waiting to meet me? Surely your trip was admirably quick?' His hint of indolent surprise and the tilt of one slashing eyebrow gave him an air of smug superiority.

'Oh, it was.' Mina looked down and flicked lint from her sleeve. 'Admirably so. Why, I didn't even have time to check my diary for commitments that might clash before I was whisked away. Or to arrange for someone to keep an eye on my apartment.'

She let her brow pucker in a frown. 'I hope the fruit I bought doesn't spoil while I'm away. And the milk.' She let her smile widen. 'But I understand. I'm sure you're used to wanting something and having it happen immediately. No time to waste on boring niceties like invitations or queries about whether the dates suited me.'

Below his rumpled black hair grooves corrugated that wide brow. Mina raised her hand. 'Not that it matters. I know how terribly valuable your time is. After all, what could I *possibly* have scheduled that could be nearly as important?'

From behind her Mina heard a snuffle from Henri that sounded suspiciously like a stifled laugh. Then he excused himself, murmuring something about putting her luggage away and prudently followed his wife down a corridor.

Which left Mina alone with Alexei Katsaros.

He didn't even seem to notice Marie and Henri leave. All his attention was on Mina.

If she were in the mood to feel fear it would have swamped her now, for the man watched her with the hyperawareness of a hunter. Then there was the sheer size of him, not only tall but well-built, all muscled strength beneath those straight shoulders. She'd caught a glimpse of a well-developed chest and taut abdominals that confirmed this man did far more than sit behind a desk, making money. His thighs beneath the faded jeans were those of a skier or a horseman, honed hard and strong.

Without taking his eyes off her, he slowly finished buttoning his white shirt. Then he tucked it into his faded jeans with a casual insouciance utterly at odds with the speculative gleam in his dark eyes.

Mina's manufactured smile solidified as he took his time shoving the material down, his hand disappearing behind the denim. For reasons she couldn't fathom the sight of him dressing made her pulse quicken. Her palm prickled as if her own hand slid down that flat abdomen.

'I'm sorry, did my arrival wake you?' The snap in her words betrayed her discomfort but Mina compensated for it by slowly taking stock of his tousled black hair and the dark shadow of beard growth across that solid jaw.

His hands fell to his sides and he stepped out of the shadows. The light hit sharply defined cheekbones, a well-shaped mouth and a stern blade of nose, down which he surveyed her. Mina was reminded of precious icons she'd seen. But whereas those old saints had looked flat and unreal, this man exuded raw energy and the glint in his dark eyes was anything but unworldly. Alexei Katsaros was too…physical for sainthood. With his imposing size and posture he could model for a cavalry officer from a previous century, supercilious and deadly in a bright uniform, with a sabre at his side.

Mina repressed the warm shiver that started at the base of her spine and threatened to crawl, vertebra by vertebra, up her back.

'You know you didn't wake me. We watched each other.' His voice was both rough and dangerously soothing.

Mina couldn't explain it but he made the simple words sound almost indecent. As if they'd been naked at the time, or as if she'd watched him doing something—

'So, you're concerned about your groceries, is that right?' One dark eyebrow rose and it took a second for Mina to follow the change of subject. She was still lost in a hazy daydream of Alexei Katsaros stripping his shirt away and reaching for the button on his jeans. 'I can have one of my staff deal with your apartment, Ms Carter, since I put you to such inconvenience.'

Mina wrenched her thoughts back to the man before her. The man whose satisfied smile told her he knew he'd unsettled her. Whose tone conveyed that she'd managed to needle him with her pointed comments about being dragged away.

'That's very kind, Mr Katsaros.' She blinked up at him, mimicking Carissa, then thought better of it. She'd never batted her eyelashes in her life and wasn't about to start.

'Something in your eye, Ms Carter?' Not by a whisker did he betray a smile yet Mina knew he laughed at her.

To her surprise, Mina had to stifle a smirk of her own. He was right. She couldn't pull off such feminine wiles. She was better to stick at being herself.

'Sand, probably.' She blinked again. 'My own fault. I insisted on driving with the window down to enjoy the breeze.'

Carissa would have shrieked at the thought of her hair getting messed up, but Alexei Katsaros didn't know that. Mina would have to get by with pretending to be a Mina version of Carissa. Less fluttery and uncertain, less overtly feminine, less willing to be bullied.

'Thank you for the offer to take care of my apartment but I prefer not to have my home taken over by strangers. I'm sure you understand.'

He understood all right. His smugness fled as he registered that she referred to his staff who'd politely yet inexorably ushered her from Carissa's flat.

'My staff disturbed you? You felt threatened in some way?' His voice was sharp.

Had he really thought she'd be happy, herded by armed bodyguards?

Mina remembered Carissa's tears and frantic fear. How would she have coped, confronting those big men with cold eyes and suave suits?

They'd been impeccably solicitous but Mina read in them the same quality she'd seen in her father's royal guards. Beneath the polish were men trained to use force. If she'd refused to go, they'd have bundled her onto that private jet without a qualm.

'Oh, I didn't feel at all threatened by anyone else while I was with them.' She paused, letting him absorb her words. Would he understand *they'd* been the threat?

His expression didn't alter.

Clearly he had no idea how frightening it was for a woman not used to close personal protection to have stony-faced men wearing shoulder holsters usher her into an anonymous vehicle.

Suddenly weary, Mina suppressed a sigh. What was the point? He wouldn't care even if he understood.

'Your staff were polite and incredibly...efficient. I'm sure no express parcel could have been delivered to your door more quickly.'

She looked away, letting her gaze rove the white marble foyer, taking in the carved Cycladic figurine in a niche on the far wall. Mina's pulse quickened with interest but she couldn't afford to be distracted. Slowly she turned back to her host, whose hands, she noticed, were bunched in fists at his sides.

He stepped forward and Mina's nape prickled.

This close she realised those intent eyes were a stunning dark green, opaque and intriguing. She'd never seen the like. Momentarily she was mesmerised. Then she dragged her thoughts back to their conversation.

'I prefer to make my own arrangements, Mr Katsaros. I'm sure you understand.'

Alexei understood all right.

He was being taken to task by a woman who didn't know she was playing with fire. Or did she believe she could set her own rules because he contemplated marriage?

That had to be it. There was no other explanation.

He'd wondered if Carter's daughter was a spoiled princess. As far as he could tell, she'd lived for years off her father's, and by extension his own, largesse, while enjoying a dilettante's life.

Now he had his answer. Carissa Carter was used to getting her own way. Spoiled rotten, he had no doubt. Her father had led her to expect an advantageous match and she seemed sure it would happen.

Yet her words disturbed him. Had she really been frightened of his security staff? Alexei barely noticed them now, just considered them a normal part of life.

He stared down at the woman who continued to surprise him. It wasn't only her plain outfit, or the accent that wasn't quite as he'd heard it over the phone, but then there'd been interference on the line. He'd imagined someone more eager to ingratiate herself. More overtly charming.

Carissa Carter was more complex than he'd imagined.

She was confident yet not in the way of a woman used to trading on male admiration. She carried herself with an intrinsic elegance that, when she looked down that straight nose at him, bordered on condescension. That intrigued. As did the intelligence shining in those sherry-coloured eyes and in the snarky undercurrent of her conversation.

He'd imagined Carter's daughter more eminently dismissible. The man had said her nature was sweet rather than incisive and that she wasn't cut out for business. Alexei had assumed she was pretty but vacuous.

How wrong he'd been.

Nor was she as he'd expected her to look. He saw no resemblance to Carter in her dark hair, luminous eyes or expressive mouth. Her skin was golden, not pale, and she met his gaze with a direct curiosity that, at any other time, he'd appreciate.

It evoked a hungry gnawing in the pit of his belly, a reminder that, despite his preoccupation with her father, Alexei was a vigorous man with healthy appetites.

He drew a slow breath, marshalling his thoughts, and was fascinated to see that, despite her sugared verbal barbs, Carissa Carter wasn't immune to him after all. Her eyes tracked the rise of his chest, her pupils dilating as if mesmerised. Then she blinked and turned away, feigning indifference.

Satisfaction stirred. He'd disliked her jabs about the way he'd got her here, had even felt a stirring of remorse. Seeing that chink in her armour pleased him.

'How remiss of me to keep a guest standing in the foyer.' Alexei smiled and watched a tiny wrinkle appear above the bridge of her nose, as if she concentrated on not reacting. Fascinating.

'Won't you come in?' He stood aside and gestured for her to precede him into the main sitting room.

'Thank you.' She inclined her head in the slightest nod.

Alexei caught a hint of perfume as she passed. Another surprise. He'd expected some expensive designer scent but this was one he'd never encountered. Instead of florals or cloying sweetness, she'd chosen a fragrance that hinted at the exotic Near East. Alexei inhaled cinnamon and spice and a warm, earthy richness that made him think, bizarrely, of veiled temptresses in gauzy silks. He canted towards her.

Fortunately she didn't notice. She entered the sitting room with that leisurely, swaying stroll that spoke of casual confidence. As if she were accustomed to a billionaire's luxury lifestyle. But then, given her father's thievery...

He watched as she caught sight of the ancient sculpture against one wall. The torso of a young man, the musculature and veining of chest and arms superbly executed, the filmy fabric of his tunic the work of a master. She stiffened and drew a sharp breath. A second later she stood before the ruined masterpiece, her hand stretching momentarily towards it before dropping to her side.

'It's magnificent.' There was genuine awe in her words. Alexei recognised it. He felt the same way about the piece.

His mouth twisted. Despite all expectation

he found Carissa Carter…refreshing. Perhaps it wouldn't be so tough pretending to be interested in her till her father arrived.

'It was discovered at the bottom of the sea.'

As if his words broke the spell of artistic appreciation, she spun around, that oversized black T-shirt swirling wide. What did she look like beneath it? The rest of her was slim and beautifully formed.

'You have a very nice home, Mr Katsaros.' Her voice appealed too. It was low and musical. Not high and breathy as he recalled it from the phone call. Though he'd probably taken her by surprise with his invitation.

Alexei's mouth tightened. She was right. It had been a demand, not an invitation. Carissa had made him sound brutish and that annoyed him. But the situation demanded a swift resolution. He didn't have time for niceties.

Her eyebrows arched when he didn't respond to her small talk.

'Call me Alexei.'

'Thank you, Alexei.' Her voice slowed on his name and he felt the oddest sensation, as if she'd reached out one slim hand and trailed it down his chest, right to his belly. Abdominal muscles clenched in response. 'Please, call me Carissa.'

'Carissa.' He tested the sibilant on his tongue and saw her eyes darken. The sight sent another ripple of awareness through him. She was definitely attracted. 'You have an interesting accent. Not the same as your father's.'

Intriguingly she stiffened as if he'd hit a weak point. It was the tiniest movement but unmistakeable to a man who'd spent so long studying the vulnerabilities of business opponents.

'My father's accent is English. But we moved around a lot when I was young. I suppose mine's a hybrid.'

Alexei watched the unblinking way she held his gaze and wondered what she hid.

'Yours is interesting too.' She spoke quickly, clearly wanting to divert his attention.

Alexei was interested to find that despite his fixation on locating and punishing her father, his curiosity about Carissa increased by the moment.

He gestured for her to take a seat and sank down onto a leather lounge, crossing his ankles and leaning back.

'Russian mother, Greek father, moved to London as a kid.' He shrugged. 'Like yours, my accent's a hybrid.' More like mongrel, he silently corrected. He'd spent too long living precariously in places where the predominant language was

that of the violent gangs who ruled through in-
timidation.

Silently Carissa nodded and sat opposite him.
In contrast to her casual clothes her posture was
graceful. With that long, slender neck and perfect
poise he was reminded again of a dancer sweep-
ing into a low curtsey. He could picture a tiara
on her smooth, dark hair and a sheaf of flowers
in her arms.

'Tell me, Carissa, have you heard from your
father?'

'He's not here?' Her expression flickered but
too fast for him to read it.

'No, but I'm expecting him soon.' As soon as
Ralph Carter heard his precious daughter was
staying at Alexei's private island he'd hotfoot it
here, hoping the marriage he'd suggested would
save him from Alexei's wrath. If that didn't work,
Alexei had the perfect hostage to lure him from
hiding.

'I see.' She chewed the corner of her mouth and
then, as if aware of his scrutiny, offered a small
smile. 'That will be lovely.' Once more her direct
look suggested she hid something. What?

'So you haven't heard from him?'

'No. He seems to have his phone switched off.
Do you need to contact him urgently?'

Alexei fought impatience. His desire for retribution against the one person he'd actually *trusted* in decades hadn't eased. Fury curdled his gut. He couldn't believe he'd been foolish enough to let Carter con him.

'Not at all. In the meantime we can get to know each other better.' That prospect grew more enticing by the moment.

She shifted in her seat, her first overt sign of nervousness. Intrigued, Alexei took his time surveying her, his fingers tracing a lazy circle on the soft leather of his chair's arm.

'I want you to be happy here, Carissa. Let me know if there's anything you want.'

'That's very kind of you, Alexei. For that matter, very kind of you to let me holiday here in this glorious place.'

She'd changed her tune. Fifteen minutes ago she'd been complaining about his staff and the speed with which he'd brought her here. What had changed?

Every sense stirred. He scented not fear but caution, as if Carissa suddenly felt out of her depth. Not so sure of herself after all?

She wasn't his target; her father was. Yet that didn't stop a frisson of satisfaction at the suggestion Ms high and mighty Carter had second thoughts about her situation. If she was cast in the same mould as her father, it would do her no harm to learn she couldn't have everything her way. Especially if she'd spent the past few years living off money her father had stolen from Alexei.

'Oh, I don't consider it a kindness, given our special situation.'

She stilled. It looked as if she didn't even breathe. 'Our special situation?'

'Of course.' This time Alexei's smile was genuine. 'Since we're marrying.'

CHAPTER THREE

MINA'S MOUTH DRIED as she watched a slow smile transform Alexei's face. It wasn't a polite expression of friendship or amusement. It was a wide grin that she could only describe as dangerous.

More than that. *Hungry.* As if he wanted to sink those strong white teeth into her flesh.

She shivered as heat licked through her. Disgust, of course. She wasn't some dish served up to satisfy his appetite.

Yet, on the thought, Mina realised her response wasn't so simple. A shiver drew her breasts tight till her nipples beaded. Astonished, she realised she was torn between annoyance and excitement.

As if she *wanted* to satisfy Alexei Katsaros's animal appetites. And hers, as well.

The realisation had her fingers clawing the arms of her chair as she fought the urge to reel back. As much at her own confusing reaction as at his overtly *masculine* perusal. He surveyed her like a man who'd just bought a woman.

She despised him. Yet despite her outrage, Mina felt a thrill of anticipation.

By the time she'd conquered her shock, there was no sign of that feral hunger in his expression. Had she imagined it?

Mina wasn't an expert on sex but she'd had her share of admirers. Men whom she found it easy to resist. For some reason they were fine as friends, but when they wanted more, Mina didn't. Yet she knew what sexual interest looked like.

She couldn't see it in his face now.

'We've only just met.' Her tone was cool.

One dark eyebrow rose. 'It was your father's suggestion that we'd make a good match. He told me you'd agreed. Are you saying that's not the case?'

Mina swallowed, ignoring the sandpaper abrasion of her throat, and wondered how best to play for time. All the way here she'd told herself Carissa had been mistaken and that Alexei Katsaros couldn't want *marriage*. He didn't need to marry a stranger. He was rich, successful and good-looking.

Also impatient, determined and self-obsessed, if his idea of finding a wife was ordering her to his island and giving her no choice!

What had she landed herself in? Surely he hadn't brought her here for a wedding!

Shock jagged through her, stealing her breath. If so, then this masquerade would be over before it began. Mina forced herself to take a deep breath and think.

'He did mention a possible marriage, but...'

'But?'

'We don't know each other! I can't agree to marry someone I don't know.'

He said nothing, just crossed his arms, the movement drawing Mina's attention to the depth of his broad chest and the muscled power of his biceps. He was a man whose physical size and fitness could daunt a woman who wasn't strong enough to stand up for herself.

'So you're here to what? Get to know me?'

'Is that so unreasonable?' Mina jumped on the idea like a lifeline. 'We're talking about a lifetime commitment.'

The hint of a smile flickered at the corner of Alexei's mouth. 'That's a refreshingly...old-fashioned view.'

Mina let her eyebrows climb. 'Marriage is a serious commitment. Why enter into one if you don't plan to make it work?' She wasn't sure why she didn't simply shrug off his comment. But marriage, like the right to make her own decisions, was something she felt strongly about. Her mother had married her country's Sheikh not for love but because her family decreed it. It hadn't been a happy match.

'I see your point.' Alexei nodded.

'So you understand I need time to determine if a marriage would work. Surely you want that too.'

'To assess if we're *compatible*?' Alexei didn't move, nor did his expression alter, yet the quality of that stare flicked a warning switch. Adrenalin surged in Mina's blood. Heat consumed her as if he'd surveyed every inch of her body with that searing scrutiny, instead of merely holding her gaze.

How did he do that?

More important, why did she react so?

Mina wasn't oblivious to men but she'd never been swept off her feet, or into bed, by one. Her history made her cautious about ceding control to any man. Before his death, her father had mapped out her life, giving her no choice, even about the clothes she wore and the subjects she studied. Since leaving Jeirut for Paris she'd devoted herself single-mindedly to art, determined to carve a career in the field she loved. The guys who tried to sidetrack her into a relationship had never caused a ripple in her world.

Now it wasn't a ripple she felt but an earth tremor.

Mina wouldn't let that daunt her.

She lifted one hand negligently. 'Before we worry about *compatible* perhaps we should start with finding out if we'd survive the marriage without killing each other.'

Alexei gave a crack of laughter. 'Good point, Carissa.' The light dancing in his eyes made him look completely different. Like someone she wanted to know.

Mina stiffened.

The first time she'd seen Alexei Katsaros, something happened that had never happened before. Her certainty had wavered and with it her confidence. Mina couldn't abide the idea of being tentative around him, like some gullible, awed girl. It was easier to confront him. She suspected if he exerted himself to be nice it would be too easy to feel the force of his charm.

Now, abruptly, as she met his smiling look, the events of the last twelve hours took their toll.

Exhaustion slammed into Mina. Despite her determination not to back down before this man, she felt herself slump. Adrenalin had kept her going. Now that dissipated, leaving her overtired limbs shaky and her head swimming.

She had to get out of here before she made a mistake. Mina was too weary to guard her tongue and thinking straight became harder by the second. This man with the piercing green eyes would trip her up, especially since she wasn't practised at lying.

If he discovered the truth, all this would have been for nothing. Carissa needed time to get away with Pierre and cover her tracks.

'I'm sorry, you'll have to excuse me.' Mina lifted her hand to cover a yawn, only to discover the fake yawn was real. 'I'm suddenly very tired.'

'You didn't sleep on the flight?' He looked surprised.

Mina shook her head. She'd been ushered onto the private jet late in the evening for the overnight flight to the Caribbean. But despite the comfortable bed, she'd had too much going on in her head to sleep.

'It's been a very long day.' She glanced at her watch, trying to calculate the time difference but to her surprise, her mind was too foggy. Tiredness and stress took their toll. 'I've been awake more than twenty-four hours.' And yesterday had been a long day, even before Carissa had dragged her into this mess. Or, to be fair, since she'd thrust herself into it to protect her friend.

Time to regroup before she said something she shouldn't.

Mina pinned on a smile, the multipurpose one she reserved for royal meet and greets. She hadn't used it in years and it felt rusty. 'I'm sorry, Alexei, but I'll have to leave you for now.' She rose, surprised at the effort it took to stand tall. Her knees were unsteady, and for a second she swayed.

'Could you point me towards my room, please?'

He loomed before her, the beginnings of a frown creasing his forehead. 'You look pale.'

'I'm fine,' she lied. How many hours had it been since she'd eaten? She hadn't been in the mood for food on the plane, refuelling on coffee and lots of it, but now the caffeine had worn off and she felt as powerful as a dandelion in a strong wind. 'If you could show me the way?'

When Alexei didn't immediately answer, Mina swung round towards the entry, remembering Henri heading down a corridor from there.

As she turned, another wave of tiredness hit and her movements lost their usual precise control. Her foot caught the edge of the plush carpet.

She didn't trip or stagger, just paused, swaying as she caught her balance.

'I'll take you.' The deep voice came from beside her ear as, to her astonishment, Alexei bent and curled his arms around her back and legs. An instant later she was in the air. Or, more precisely, in his arms, pressed against a hot body that seemed to be all solid muscle.

Mina's breath stalled, then released on a shaky sigh at how extraordinary this felt. No one had ever held her like this. She registered conflicting feelings: shock, pleasure and an unexpected desire to burrow closer. As if Alexei were someone she trusted. Or desired.

'There's no need.' The words were crisp, at odds with the strange wobbly feeling in her middle. It was impossible to sit straighter and assert control when she lay in his arms, unable to get any purchase.

Alexei ignored her words, marching out of the room.

With each step Mina felt her body move against his in a swaying rhythm that was surprisingly appealing. In other circumstances...

In other circumstances this wouldn't happen, ever.

'Thank you for your consideration,' she said between barely open lips. 'But I prefer to walk.'

That made him pause. He angled his head to look down at her and Mina was bombarded with impressions. The hard perfection of his squared-off jaw. From this intriguing angle, it was a study in obstinate power. The soaring, proud cheekbones that spoke of ancient Slavic heritage. The flare of arrogant nostrils and the fly-away effect of his winged eyebrows. The steady pump of his heart against her ribs and the power of those iron-hard arms encircling her.

Something shivered to life in the pit of Mina's belly. Something that grew as she inhaled a tempting cedar-and-citrus aftershave that melded with the hot, salt scent of male skin. Her nostrils twitched appreciatively and the shiver amplified.

Astounded, Mina watched his eyes darken, the pupils dilating.

The world eclipsed to the dark mystery of that shadowy stare, heating her in all sorts of places.

When he spoke the sound vibrated from his chest into her body. She'd never experienced anything as intimate as his voice reverberating through her while his eyes devoured her.

'Relax. I'm not going to hurt you.'

Despite the certainty he wouldn't drop her, Mina couldn't ignore the inner voice screaming at her to get away. Being this close to Alexei Katsaros was perilous, whatever his stated intention.

'I prefer to walk. If you'll kindly put me down.' Tiredness vanished, replaced with quivering watchfulness.

'And have you trip and hurt yourself?' He shook his head, his rumpled locks swinging free. 'I wouldn't forgive myself.'

His tone was admirably sincere yet Mina read the tiny creases at the corners of his mouth and knew he was enjoying himself. Could he feel her heart hammer? She hated being vulnerable to him.

Before she could read any more, he looked away and began walking down the hall, carrying her easily, as if he carted unwilling women around every day.

Maybe he did.

'Contrary to what you might have heard, Mr Katsaros, women are capable of thinking for themselves. We don't appreciate he-men making our decisions for us. I—'

'Is that what you think I am?' Annoyingly his pace didn't falter. 'What exactly does that mean?' His jaw jutted as he ruminated. 'Someone very masculine? Someone who sees an exhausted guest and looks after her so she doesn't hurt herself?'

Mina counted to ten. If she thought it would do any good, she'd struggle against his hold. But, though fit, she was no match for all that hard-packed muscle, especially given his superior size. He was well over six feet. If Alexei Katsaros didn't want to release her she couldn't make him. The knowledge infuriated her and she began stringing together curses in her own language that she couldn't say lest he wonder how she knew Arabic.

She forced her gaze away from that annoyingly superior chin, focusing on the play of light and shadow on the ceiling as they passed down the hall.

'After all,' he continued, 'as you pointed out so eloquently, it was my fault your trip was so… precipitate. If I'd been more conscious of your comfort I'd have organised for you to travel during the day, or ensured the bed on the plane was more comfortable. I'll have it replaced.'

'There's no need for that. The bed was quite comfortable.' Even to her ears her voice sounded thin. She held on to her temper by a tiny margin. All her life she'd been taught not to reveal anger. This time she dared not lose control because he'd see it as a victory.

'Then it's a wonder you didn't sleep. Perhaps—' she caught movement in her peripheral vision and turned to see him send a teasing look her way '—you couldn't sleep because you were excited about visiting me.'

Excited! About as excited as if she visited a zoo to see a rattlesnake. Mina sucked in a rough breath, then stilled as the movement made her more aware of Alexei's big hand on her ribs, close to her breast.

'Perhaps I didn't sleep because I was busy contacting people to reschedule things for the period I'll be away. Since I had no opportunity earlier.' She slanted him a frosty stare only to find that smile lurking around his mouth.

'Ah, yes, no doubt your agenda is full of priority appointments.' His expression didn't change but his tone revealed how unlikely he thought it.

Mina didn't bother to disabuse him. She might not run a multinational corporation, but nor was she idle. As well as the exhibition she was preparing for, she volunteered with disabled kids and at a nearby nursing home, doing art therapy. Plus, there was some admin work at a women's shelter, the latest design commission for the perfumery in Jeirut and another from a French company that had seen her perfume bottle designs and wanted something similar.

'Mr Katsaros.' Her patience was perilously close to failing. One more jibe and she'd forget her resolve. 'I really must—

'Alexei, remember?' His voice rumbled through her like an intimate caress. It was the final straw.

'Put. Me. Down.' Her voice rose from request to imperious command. 'Now!'

Mina caught a flash of white teeth, a glimpse of glinting eyes and suddenly the world fell away as she dropped from his arms.

'As you wish, Princess.' He spoke as she landed with a puff of expelled air on her back. She was on a bed, looking up into dark, laughing eyes. But Mina was too tired and stressed to be amused. She didn't appreciate being the butt of his jibes or his arrogant certainty that her life was of negligible importance.

Mina jackknifed to a sitting position, swiping a cushion off the bed with one hand and throwing it in the same, fluid movement. She had the satisfaction of seeing it hit him square on his superior chin.

'Be thankful that wasn't anything heavier. My aim is as good as any man's.' She heaved a breath that, to her horror, felt far too shaky. 'Now, if you'd have the decency to leave, I'd like to catch up on some much-needed sleep.'

Damn. Damn. Damn.

Alexei stalked away from the guest wing to the master suite.

What had got into him? Half an hour with Carissa Carter and he'd veered between anger, attraction, approval and amusement. And far too much of all of them. He always controlled his emotions; he wasn't undercut by them.

He hadn't expected to be impressed by Carter's precious princess. He'd been ready to write her off as a pampered bimbo who viewed the world through the prism of her greed for an easy life. Instead he'd discovered someone witty, incisive, challenging and sexy. Ridiculously sexy, given her defiantly unfeminine clothes.

On Carissa Carter even a baggy T-shirt and leggings made his hormones surge. And that mouth. She was sharp-tongued in a superior way that made him want to take her mouth and discover what sweetness lay beneath its cutting edge.

There was definitely sweetness. He'd been surprised, when he held her, at the fretful way her pulse raced. He'd been mesmerised by her contrary reactions as she pretended not to respond. Her breathing had quickened, her pupils dilated, and he'd read confusion beneath her scorn and defiance. Even her awe as she admired the sculpture in the sitting room had charmed him.

He'd lit from within at the feel of her, supple, streamlined and, he discovered, curved in the right places.

What would happen if he followed her down onto that bed? He couldn't remember the dark frenzy of desire ever being so immediate or urgent.

The very fact he'd thought about it was a concern. Did he really want an affair with Carter's daughter?

Logic demanded an unequivocal *no*. Instinct screamed *yes*.

Which was an excellent reason to pull back. Apart from the fact he didn't take advantage of vulnerable women.

Alexei rubbed a hand across his jaw as he entered his suite and crossed to the window to stand staring across the infinity pool to the sea beyond.

Guilt trickled down his spine. Bad enough that there'd been a kernel of truth in Carissa's accusation about how he'd got her here. It had solidified into a jagged shard of ice when he'd heard the hint of a wobble in her voice as she stared up at him from her bed. She'd been flushed and furious and he'd revelled in his power to rile her, till he'd heard the tiny crack in her façade of superiority. Suddenly it hadn't seemed amusing.

It hit him that he'd behaved like a kid pulling a girl's pigtails, desperate to get her attention any way he could.

Him, desperate?

Hardly. Certainly not for the likes of Carissa Carter.

Except she wasn't as he'd expected.

He scraped his hand across his chin, feeling the stubble he hadn't bothered to shave. He shouldn't allow himself to be diverted by her. She was incidental to his plans.

But, pending Carter's arrival, there wasn't much he could do to bring those plans to fruition. Steps had been taken to contain the damage, and while Alexei checked in daily, working via computer and phone, his team was working hard.

Which gave him leisure to ponder his would-be bride.

Alexei's brow scrunched. Funny. He'd assumed Carissa would be eager to marry. Her father had come up with the idea, no doubt desperate to cement personal ties that would save him when his embezzlement came to light. The fact a woman in her mid-twenties was willing to go along with such a plan pointed to her being venal, marrying for money and position.

Too many women had tried to tie him down. Not for love, but as their ticket to wealth and privilege. Alexei didn't fool himself into believing they were attracted by his character or sense of humour. Some were drawn by his looks but money was the deciding factor.

Yet Carissa hadn't given an unequivocal yes.

Why? Did she believe if he had to work for what he wanted, he'd appreciate her more? Because men enjoyed the chase?

He huffed a breath. Maybe she had something there. If she'd walked in the door and promptly agreed with everything his interest wouldn't have been piqued.

Except by that delectable body, which he'd discovered was curvier than he'd first thought.

Except for her intelligence and sensitivity.

Alexei shoved his fists in his pockets and rocked back on his feet, annoyed. He'd been so caught up in the need to draw Carter out of hiding, he hadn't bothered researching the man's daughter.

He'd acted rashly, driven by fury that the one person he'd trusted since his mother died had betrayed him.

That was a slashing wound that wouldn't heal till Carter was made to pay. It overset Alexei's equilibrium, evoking unwanted feelings that interfered with his decision-making.

It wasn't so much the money, but the personal affront of betrayal. The cold slap of horror that he'd let himself be gulled into believing the man, *liking* him.

Carter had made a fool of him, conning him into giving his trust. Not just because of the man's work qualities.

But because Carter reminded him of his father.

Like Alexei's father, Carter appeared taciturn to outsiders, but his features broke into smiles when he mentioned his family. Uncannily, Carter also had a mannerism, a tilt of the head, that echoed Alexei's precious memories of the father who'd died when Alexei was six.

Then there was his utter devotion to his spouse. There'd been no mistaking the man's devastation when his wife was diagnosed with a terminal illness. His stoic determination to do all he could for her had touched a chord with Alexei. Plus there was that unexpected weakness for silly puns and his scrupulous honesty, both hallmarks of his dad.

Alexei shook his head. Scrupulous honesty!

For years Alexei's motto had been trust no one. He and his mother had suffered because they'd been taken in by a conman. After his stepfather there'd been others, loan sharks, employers, landlords, vultures who'd preyed on his vulnerable mother, turning her life into a misery till finally loss and disappointment crushed her.

Alexei scraped a hand across his jaw, dragging himself back to the present. To the woman in one of the guest suites.

He'd acted instinctively, securing her to give him an edge. He should have ordered a dossier on her so he knew something about her before acting.

All he remembered from Carter's conversations was that she lived in Paris, where she'd attended an exclusive art school. She loved fashion and shopping and wasn't cut out for a commercial career. Alexei had gained the impression of a pampered airhead pretending to be an artist. A blonde airhead, he remembered from the photo Carter had waved before him and which he hadn't bothered to take in.

So Carissa Carter had dyed her hair. That was one extra fact about her.

Alexei considered ordering a full report on her. But why bother?

She was here. Whatever Alexei wanted to know, he'd find out for himself. He'd enjoy the process.

CHAPTER FOUR

MINA STARED AT the bathroom's enormous, full-length mirror and suppressed a groan. She looked like a stranger.

Carissa had said pink calmed her and made her feel centred. It was proof of how stressed she'd been that she'd packed only for her favourite colour. Almost everything in the case was pink. Candy pink, flesh pink, cerise, rose madder and more.

Mina's mouth curled in an unwilling laugh as she surveyed herself. She wore a candy-pink skirt with matching strappy sandals and a pale pink top with a silver logo that incorporated a highly stylised Eiffel Tower and an open book. Carissa had designed it for an indie book festival in Paris, one of her first commissions.

Had Carissa really planned to wear these clothes to visit Alexei Katsaros? If so she'd clearly had the Caribbean's casual, sunny reputation in mind, rather than any desire to dress up.

Or was her friend savvier than Mina gave her credit for? Maybe this wardrobe was her secret weapon, to prove she wasn't cut out to be a billionaire's wife.

That stifled Mina's humour.

Carissa needed her help and Mina wasn't quite as sure now about her ability to deal with her host.

Especially in a skirt that rode high on her thighs and a top that was more fitted than anything she usually wore. Mina wasn't ashamed of her body, but she covered more of it than her friend did. Plus Carissa was shorter and smaller in the bust, so the top was a snug fit. As for the miniskirt...

Mina shrugged. She had more to worry about than how much bare leg she displayed. Her only clothes were what she'd worn on the plane and the ones Carissa had packed. Besides, she was on a tropical island. Alexei Katsaros would be used to guests wearing shorts or swimsuits. Or, given his reputation and the knowing gleam in those remarkable eyes, nothing at all.

How many beautiful women had he seduced here?

Mina blinked as she caught the direction of her thoughts. *That* wasn't her concern. Deftly she caught up her long hair, winding it round and up into a tight knot at the back of her head. She jabbed in a securing pin and turned away.

If Alexei dismissed her because of her clothes, or because she wasn't the biddable woman he'd imagined, all the better. Clearly he hadn't expected her to voice her opinions or have more than a couple of brain cells to rub together.

It would be better if he concentrated on running his multibillion-dollar empire than on her. It hadn't even occurred to him that getting to know the woman he planned to marry was a good idea.

Remarkable!

Unbelievable!

What sort of man thought like that?

One who didn't expect to be questioned.

Who expected everyone to bend to his wishes.

Mina put away the hairdryer she'd used and entered the palatial bedroom where she'd slept like the dead for hours.

Her gaze rested on the bed she'd remade after her nap. Inevitably the image that filled her mind was of looking up from there into that fabulously sculpted face, into eyes alight with mockery, and knowing that physically she was at his mercy. It had infuriated Mina, for she'd had no choice but to put up with his macho posturing and derision.

That still smarted. She drew taller, pushing

her shoulders back, as she relived the scene and wished she still had the small jewelled dagger she'd worn as a ceremonial courtesy in Jeirut. It had been decorative but deadly, and Mina had insisted on knowing how to wield it. Would he have taken her more seriously if he'd known she was fully capable of looking after herself, no matter what the situation?

The idea conjured suitably satisfying images, but her smile faded as she faced the real source of her concern.

Her reaction to Alexei Katsaros.

It wasn't only fury she'd felt. He'd been *interesting*.

Lips twisting, Mina shook her head. He'd been fascinating. That combination of bold assurance and blatant sexuality would catch any woman's attention. Especially since physically his form was...pleasing. But add to that occasional glimpses of humour and penetrating understanding that punctured her initial estimate of a smug bully, and you had a man who left her unsettled.

Mina tried to tell herself the disorientation of tiredness had made her react to him. But innate honesty wouldn't let her pretend.

She had to face the truth.

She disliked Alexei Katsaros and his high-handed ways. He was exactly the sort of man to make her hackles rise. Yet he made her blood heat.

She was attracted to him.

The situation she'd rushed into for Carissa's sake became fraught with unseen snares, like the notorious patches of quicksand in the desert of her homeland.

She hadn't reckoned on anything like this when she'd blithely decided to help her friend. Dimly, she heard her father's voice in her head, the memory of his disapproval as he complained of her impulsive ways. She'd tried to make him proud, do her duty no matter how dull or out of tune with her own interests. But she'd been a source of frustration for him.

Face it, Mina. Nothing you did could satisfy your father. He didn't want a daughter who craved love, but an automaton who could be diplomatic on every occasion, no matter what the provocation.

She'd failed there, hadn't she?

Abruptly she spun on her foot and crossed to the glass doors that gave out onto a crystal pool and, beyond that, the tropical garden.

Mina's eyes were drawn to the profusion of

flowers, cadmium yellow, pale ochre and magenta. She felt the old temptation to reach for her sketchpad. To find peace by losing herself in art.

Instead she simply stood a little longer, inhaling the fragrance of salt air and unfamiliar floral perfumes, then set her shoulders and turned away. She couldn't hide forever. It was time to face her host.

She found him on a deep, shaded veranda. Overhead, a fan rotated lazily and the combination of wicker furniture and wide, wooden floorboards hinted at gracious days gone by, though the sprawling villa was modern.

Alexei sat, feet up, on a lounger, typing into a tablet. His hair was ruffled as if he'd combed his fingers through it and his shirt was open again. Mina saw the dark smattering of hair on his sculpted pectorals and jerked her gaze away.

That tiny sizzle deep inside didn't bode well. She'd felt it before, when he carried her in his arms. Now just the sight of him set it off.

Frowning, Mina surveyed the garden, trying to control feelings she couldn't fully identify. On the other side of the pool, a sculpture caught her eye.

'You're awake. Excellent.' Reluctantly Mina

turned, fixing a bland expression on her face. She'd known this would be difficult but she'd hoped her earlier response to him had more to do with fatigue than genuine attraction.

Fate was clearly laughing at her naivety.

Alexei set the tablet aside and swung his feet to the floor.

'Please don't get up on my account. You're working. I'll come back later.' She was only too happy to delay being alone with him.

'No, I've finished.' He gestured to the seats grouped around him and she had no choice but to take one.

Instead of a recliner, Mina selected an upright chair, conscious of the way her skirt rode even higher up her legs as she sat. Resisting the urge to tug her hem in a futile attempt to gain an extra few centimetres, she crossed her ankles and tucked her feet under her chair. She didn't look directly at her host but *felt* his gaze. It raked her from head to foot, then lifted again to linger on her legs and higher—

Mina swung her head up abruptly and met his enigmatic dark gaze.

Had she been wrong? She could have sworn he'd been ogling her. Or did her sensitivity about wearing Carissa's clothes make her imagine things? The way her breasts tingled—

'What would you like to drink?' As he spoke Marie rounded the corner of the veranda, as if in response to the summons of a silent bell.

'Something cold would be good.'

'Champagne? A cocktail? Gin and tonic?'

Mina glanced at her watch. Early afternoon. Obviously his usual guests indulged themselves. Mina, on the other hand, needed a clear head. Besides, she was in no mood to kick back and pretend this was a holiday. She felt too agitated around Alexei Katsaros.

'A juice would be lovely, thanks.' She smiled at Marie.

'Of course, ma'am. And I'll bring some food.'

Mina was about to protest that she wasn't hungry, then remembered she hadn't eaten in ages. She'd feel stronger after food. She'd better!

Marie turned to Alexei, a question on her face. In response he shook his head and gestured to a half-full jug of iced water. 'I'm fine.'

So he expected Mina to indulge while he stuck to cold water. Interesting. But then, he'd been working and he hadn't built a hugely successful corporation by drinking the day away. Mina shot a glance at that firm chin and those uncompromising features and guessed Alexei Katsaros was good at discipline and control. Then her gaze collided with his and the impact sent a silent shudder of reaction through her.

She suspected he was also excellent at letting go and indulging. There was a sensuality about that steady gaze that would unnerve her if she let it.

'I'm sorry I slept so long. I didn't—'

His raised hand cut her off. 'You needed the rest. I hope you slept well?' It was a simple question, the sort any host might make. Yet holding Alexei's gaze, feeling heat wash her skin, Mina tensed, conscious of undercurrents.

She took in his relaxed posture, the small smile, yet sensed concealment. One long finger drummed on the arm of his chair and there was an intensity about that stare...

'Thank you, yes. It's a very comfortable bed.'

And just like that, it hit her what this undercurrent was. Sexual attraction. Potent and perilous.

Mina blinked but kept her expression serene, despite the frenzied rush of shock. In her room she'd acknowledged the attraction, but the potency of her reaction unnerved her.

She'd been attracted to guys before. But this was a blast of lightning compared with the weak flicker of a single match. It was the mighty Khamsin wind that scoured the desert and shifted whole ridges of sand, compared with a gentle zephyr that merely rustled the leaves in a court-yard garden.

Mina sank back, forcing down shock, fear and excitement.

It was the excitement that worried her most. She'd always found it hard to resist adventure and challenge.

But not with this man. Not with a man who treated people like pawns on his personal chess-board. She'd be crazy to go there.

'I'm the one who should apologise.' His words snagged her attention. 'I'm sorry if I distressed you earlier, carrying you to your room.'

Mina felt again that powerful pulse of con-nection and refused to acknowledge it. Was he apologising for carrying her or because he'd rec-ognised how close she'd come to losing command of herself? Please, not the latter!

She inclined her head. 'You were concerned for me. I understand.' It didn't excuse the delib-erate way he'd goaded her, but there was no point going over that again. 'I have a favour to ask.'

'Ask away.' He sat forward and Mina sensed he'd been waiting for this.

'Can I borrow a vehicle? There are some things I need to buy.' Like underwear. Mina drew the line at wearing Carissa's lacy thongs.

'I'm afraid that's not possible.'

Mina's eyebrows lifted. Was he really so petty as to deny her transport? 'You don't trust me with your vehicle?' She'd learned to drive on unpaved mountain roads and desert dunes. She'd bet she could handle a four-wheel drive better than him.

'It's more the lack of shops that's the problem.'

'Lack of shops?'

'There aren't any. We get supplies by boat. It's not easy to indulge in retail therapy here.' He spread his hands and Mina caught the ghost of a smile. She recognised the same teasing amusement she'd seen when he'd provoked her. Had Carissa's reputation as a bargain shopaholic preceded her? Her friend was always searching for second-hand items to transform.

What exactly did Alexei know of the woman he planned to marry? So far it seemed he expected her to be obedient, possibly unintelligent and good at spending money. It was a distorted picture of Mina's friend, and didn't recommend her as a wife.

Which begged the question, why marry her?

More and more, the idea of an arranged marriage between him and Carissa seemed odd.

'Carissa?'

'Sorry?' She blinked. She'd missed what he said.

'If you need hygiene products, talk to Marie. She also has a supply of suncream and spare hats for visitors.'

Mina's smile was perfunctory. She refused to feel embarrassed by his assumption. 'Thanks, but that's not what I had in mind.'

'Later in the week, when your father's here, we'll go to one of the larger islands and you can visit the boutiques.'

Didn't that sound like fun? Steadfastly Mina yanked her mind from the inevitable scene when her masquerade was uncovered. She hoped Carissa and Pierre were safely married by then.

'Surely I could take the boat before that? This afternoon perhaps?'

'You're that desperate?' Alexei angled his head as if to survey her better. His expression didn't alter, but the flare of his nostrils hinted at impatience. 'I'm afraid not. The boat's being repaired.' Mina opened her mouth, but before she could ask he added, 'It will be available again in a day or two. I'm sure you'll enjoy an outing to the boutiques after that. I'm assured they stock an excellent range.'

'I can't wait.' Mina manufactured a smile and sank back in her seat. She didn't need a high-end boutique that catered for the rich at play. But there was no point explaining that. For now she'd simply wash her underwear every night.

Inevitably her thoughts jagged back to her unmasking when Carissa's father arrived. Her stomach squeezed uncomfortably.

She could almost hear her own father's pained voice, telling her she'd been reckless and headstrong. That she shouldn't have dared to disrupt a father's plans for his daughter.

But how could she regret helping her friend? She couldn't sit and watch her forced into marriage.

Mina wasn't afraid of Alexei's reaction when he discovered the truth, or Mr Carter's. After all, what could they do to her? And it served them right for putting Carissa in such an invidious position. Yet now the first rush of indignation on her friend's behalf was fading, Mina wasn't looking forward to the moment of revelation. It would be uncomfortable at best, especially as she relied on Alexei's goodwill to get off the island. He was bound to be furious.

What would an angry Alexei Katsaros be like? Loud and belligerent, or icily condemning?

Mina could withstand anything he threw at her. That went without saying. Yet she found herself wishing she were back in Paris, busy working instead of playing this cat-and-mouse game.

Suddenly the lack of underwear seemed the least of her concerns.

CHAPTER FIVE

ALEXEI TRIED AND failed to read Carissa's expression. She seemed distracted, almost uninterested, as if her need to shop wasn't urgent after all. He couldn't get a handle on her. Every time she confirmed his estimation of her as shallow and opportunistic, she confounded him.

Marie served drinks and a substantial platter of food but Carissa barely touched the lavish spread.

'You'll be glad to see your father again.'

Her soft eyes widened as if in surprise, and Alexei felt his own narrow.

What was going on? Had father and daughter fallen out? Surely not. If it appeared Carissa was on the verge of securing a marriage with Alexei, her father would be eager to give the match his blessing.

'Of course.'

'It's been a while since you saw each other?'

'A while.' She shifted in her seat, crossing her legs. Despite his determination to ferret out her motivations, Alexei was distracted by the toned golden skin on display. The ploy of a woman bent on seduction? Why else would she wear a micro miniskirt and a tight top that so lovingly moulded her breasts?

Unwanted heat flared as he considered the generous bounty barely concealed by Carissa's new clothes. How had he thought her lacking in curves? She was slender yet definitely feminine. And those legs went on forever.

Yet when he dragged his gaze to her face, she was staring, not at him but towards the horizon, her brow knitted in thought.

Alexei experienced an odd sensation, a clamping in his gut. It took a moment to realise it was pique. He wasn't used to being ignored by anyone, especially women.

Especially a woman who thought she was here to marry him.

Was Carissa so sure of herself that she didn't feel the need to pander to his ego?

She turned her head, her gaze meshing with his, and his blood pumped powerfully. How would it feel if she reached out and touched him? The notion quickened his pulse to a hard, heavy throb.

'Something's on your mind.' His voice was rough. 'What is it?'

She blinked, as if surprised at his words. For a second he almost believed he'd unsettled her, though that was unlikely. When she'd arrived she'd been very vocal. There'd been nothing reticent or uncertain about Carissa. He'd enjoyed their sparring. It was rare Alexei had someone confront him, much less take him to task for his actions.

Carissa seemed to gather herself. She sat higher, those slim shoulders forming a straight, uncompromising line that even after such a short acquaintance was familiar. Her jaw angled up and Alexei felt anticipation thrum.

'Why do you want an arranged marriage? Why not marry someone you know?'

Again she surprised him. He hadn't suspected Carter's daughter would look a gift horse in the mouth. But clearly Carissa was intelligent. Even if she craved his wealth, she wanted to understand his expectations.

'I haven't found anyone I want to marry.' That, at least, was true.

'But why arrange a marriage this way?'

'Are you trying to back out?' He sat forward, fascinated.

'No.' She paused. 'I just want to know more about you.'

'It seemed an efficient way of proceeding.'

'Efficient?' She tilted her head and recrossed her legs.

He heard the faint sibilant whisper of fabric on skin and fought to keep his eyes on her face. If she thought he'd be distracted by the obvious tactic she was mistaken, but that didn't prevent arousal clamping his groin.

'You make it sound as easy as ordering from a catalogue.' She gestured dismissively. 'Wanted, one female of reasonable appearance and education. Must have all her own teeth and be of child-bearing age.' She snapped the words out, and again Alexei heard that edge of disapproval. Yet instead of annoying him, it stirred a desire to provoke more of the same. Heat simmered in his blood at the idea of Carissa aroused to heightened emotion.

If he had to wait for her father to come out of hiding, he might as well enjoy himself.

'Why not? Look what it's brought me.' He let his gaze drop, trailing down her long, proud neck to her collarbone, the high curve of her breasts and lower.

Her fingers dug into the arms of her chair, the tendons in the backs of her hands tensing.

'And since you mention child-bearing...' He

lifted his eyes to hers. They blazed back at him with a banked fury that might have made him pause in other circumstances. He didn't want Carissa calm and dismissive or, worse, distracted. He preferred her hot under the collar, concentrating on *him*. 'How do you feel about starting a family straight away?'

'That's why you want to marry? To have children?' Surprising how stunned she sounded. Surely the thought of kids must have occurred to her?

Alexei shrugged. 'Why else? When I have children I want them to have my name, to be part of a family unit. There's nothing else I can get from marriage that I can't have already.'

Alexei *did* want a family. Kids of his own. He'd spent years driven by the need to drag himself out of poverty and hadn't looked beyond securing success and financial security. Determination had kept him climbing to the top. But one day, yes, a family of his own...

He had a few precious memories of happy family life before his father died but he knew how lucky he was to have those. The miserable years after his mother remarried made him appreciate what he'd had so briefly. He'd like to recreate that with his own children.

When this debacle with Carter was over he'd think of finding a woman suitable to share his life. Someone who'd make a wonderful mother.

'There's nothing else you can get from marriage?' Carissa's mouth twisted superciliously. 'How about emotional intimacy? Trust? Love?'

'Love?' He frowned. 'You believe in love?'

Yet she was happy to sell herself into a marriage of convenience. The woman was a mass of contradictions.

Carissa hesitated. Her hands plucked at the arm of her chair. 'I believe it exists,' she said eventually.

'But you've never been in love.' It was a guess, but Alexei always backed his hunches. The idea intrigued, that a pretty woman in her mid-twenties had never fancied herself in love.

'Have *you*?' She raised one eyebrow.

'No.' People talked of love but it was rare.

His parents had married for love and he admitted the idea held allure. But look where it had left his mother. When Alexei's father died she'd been heartbroken. Even as a young child he'd understood that. She'd forced herself to go through the motions of life but she'd never been the same. Her sense of loss had been behind her disastrous second marriage. She'd admitted it to

Alexei before she died and he'd had to bite back a howl of protest that she hadn't been alone. She'd had *him*. But clearly that hadn't been enough. *He* hadn't been enough.

Almost as bad, it turned out her other reason for remarrying was to provide Alexei with a father. Because of that she'd condemned them to life with that miserable excuse for a man.

Futile anger boiled in his belly. Alexei wouldn't let anyone make him weak the way his mother had been.

He'd triumphed over adversity and made himself a man his father would have been proud of. He had no intention of falling into some sentimental trap.

'So you don't expect to love the woman you marry.'

Carissa's cool tone cleaved his thoughts. She surveyed him with faint disapproval.

'If you're waiting for a declaration from me, Princess, you'll be disappointed.'

Predictably she didn't bat an eye. This woman had grit.

'What if you fall in love with someone else after you marry?'

'I can't imagine it happening.' Alexei saw her open her mouth to object and raised a hand. 'But if, after some time, we divorce, you needn't be concerned. The legal agreement will ensure you're recompensed.'

Her jaw inched even higher. 'And if your wife fell for someone else?'

Alexei met her challenging stare and felt a tiny beat of surprise. At the idea of the woman he married preferring another man. And at Carissa's determination to speak in the abstract. As if discussing some faceless woman instead of herself.

Why did she pretend lack of interest when she was here for marriage? Even now, staring along the length of that straight nose like a monarch surveying a vulgar yokel, she couldn't hide her awareness of him. Alexei read her shortened breathing, the pebbled nipples pressing invitingly against taut fabric. He understood, with the experience of a man who'd attracted women since his teens, that Carissa was anything but uninterested.

The knowledge sent a frisson down his spine, to circle his body and lodge in his groin.

Carissa Carter might be a necessary encumbrance for now but increasingly Alexei recognised a woman he'd enjoy knowing better.

Perhaps when his business with her father was

resolved they might come to a mutually enjoyable arrangement.

'You want to bring children into a family where there's no love, just a…commercial agreement?' Carissa's tone jabbed through his pleasant imaginings. 'Don't you think that's selfish?'

Alexei frowned. 'Children need stability.' His own childhood was a case in point. 'They'd have the love of their parents, and a caring, settled environment. That's more than many kids ever have.'

He took in the flat line of her mouth and the opaque look in her eyes, and wondered what Carissa was thinking. Had his words struck a chord?

Yet she'd been one of the lucky ones. The Carters had been a tight-knit family. There'd been no mistaking Ralph Carter's devastation over his wife's death, or his concern for his daughter.

Alexei recalled the late-night conversation he'd had with Carter after his wife's death. Alexei had been leaving his office and been surprised to see the older man still in the building, though his glazed eyes had told their own story. Alexei had taken a seat, unable to walk past the man, reading the small, telltale signs of fiercely suppressed emotion.

In that moment Ralph Carter had reminded

him of his father, who, while devoted to his family, closely guarded deep emotions. Alexei had known he was loved, not by words but by his father's actions.

That night Alexei had felt a bond to Carter, enough to unbend and admit he'd count himself lucky to have a marriage such as Carter had enjoyed. It had been a moment of unfamiliar, unguarded sentimentality that surprised him.

No wonder Carter's subsequent betrayal stuck in his craw. For the first time in his life Alexei had opened up about his most private desires, while trying to help the other man. He'd felt a brief moment of shared understanding. Then a couple of months later the guy had ripped him off, proving Alexei's trust had been totally misplaced.

Not only that. Carter remembered Alexei's admission that since he'd never have a love match, he'd settle for marriage based on respect and common goals. Carter had tried to exploit that. Last week, before his embezzlement was uncovered, he'd suggested Alexei consider marrying his daughter. He'd described her as beautiful, gentle and generous, if impractical at building a career.

Alexei gritted his teeth. Clearly she wasn't impractical enough to resist the lure of marriage to a billionaire.

'So, Carissa,' he drawled. 'You're not in favour of marriage without love, but here you are on my private island. Why?'

She curled her fingers into the arms of her chair, discomfited. Then she shrugged, the movement making those lush breasts jiggle. 'I didn't say I'm not in favour of it. But I like to know where I stand, hence my questions.'

Alexei sat forward. 'Where *do* you stand, Carissa? Do you want to marry me and have my babies?'

Strange how saying it jolted heat through his belly. At the thought of Carissa in his bed. He had no trouble imagining that lissom body beneath his or astride it or against the wall of the shower as he took her with the water streaming over them. As for her pregnant with his baby— Alexei was stunned by the heavy whump of desire that slammed into him.

Carissa Carter was lovely to look at but far from the most beautiful woman he'd met. She was mouthy and opinionated, avaricious enough to marry a stranger for money. Yet, after knowing her mere hours, Alexei wanted her in his bed.

Had his wits taken a hike?

She sat back in her seat, taking time to recross her legs. Was the seat uncomfortable, or was she nervous?

More likely she was employing the not-so-subtle means of drawing his attention to her stunning legs.

Did she think he'd be so mesmerised she could manipulate him when they negotiated a prenuptial agreement?

'The jury's still out, Alexei. Surely you don't expect me to make up my mind within a couple of hours of meeting you.'

He applauded her aplomb. Her answer was designed to buy her time, and improve her bargaining position, making him more eager to seal the deal. It worked. Though there was no marriage contract to seal, Alexei felt his interest quicken. He'd always found it hard to resist a challenge.

'What if I don't want to wait?'

Her dark eyebrows arched. 'Then perhaps I'm not the woman you need. I'm happy to return to Paris…' She let the words hang but shuffled forward in her seat as if ready to get up and go right then and there.

As if he'd let her go! She was his bargaining chip. The reason Ralph Carter would believe it safe to come out of hiding.

If Carter baulked at showing himself, there were other possibilities. The man doted on Carissa. All Alexei had to do was suggest he'd make the daughter pay for her father's sins, in his bed, since she didn't have money, and Carter would come running to her rescue.

'No. You'll stay here, where we can get to know each other better.'

Did he imagine she tensed? Then she shrugged and the illusion vanished. 'That sounds ideal. I'm sure neither of us want to make a mistake on such a significant...'

'Merger?'

Fascinated, Alexei watched the faintest tinge of pink colour her cheeks. Was she thinking, as he was, of their bodies merging in the most intimate of ways?

'Decision.' Carissa's voice was crisp. She reached out and took a bread stick from the platter, broke it in half and crunched.

Alexei suppressed a laugh and reached for a piece of Marie's fried chicken. The delicious aroma made him inhale appreciatively.

'I look forward to getting to know you better, Carissa. And as for the question of starting a family immediately—' her eyes locked on his '—we can negotiate.'

She inclined her head slightly, the picture of cool condescension.

Which made Alexei want to ruffle her composure all the more. The urge to reach out to her made his fingers tingle but he refused to follow through. No matter how enjoyable that would be, he needed to keep his eye on the main game.

It was almost a shame that this was all a front. He'd enjoy negotiating with Carissa over sex. Perhaps he *would* see if she was interested in an affair when this was over.

Except by then her father would be ruined and in prison. It was unlikely she'd want anything to do with Alexei after that.

Reluctantly Alexei decided the best thing for now was to keep things low-key. He'd treat her as a guest rather than a prospective bride. He didn't need the complications that would follow if he acted on this attraction.

'When you've finished eating, I'll show you around.'

Mina enjoyed Alexei's voice, she realised. Its deep, suede quality was compelling. Worse, it weakened her, as if he brushed her flesh with plush fur that invited her to arch against it. There was his accent too. His English was crisp enough to prove it wasn't his first language; he had rich, round vowels, and the occasional soft consonant gave his voice a seductive quality.

Or perhaps he did that deliberately. He'd been toying with her, occasionally flirting as they spoke.

To see how she responded? Or because that was the nature of the man?

All she knew for sure was that Carissa had had a lucky escape. She'd have been miserable with Alexei, a man who viewed finding a wife as a matter of efficiency, and no doubt the woman herself as a possession!

It would do him good to discover she wasn't a chattel to be acquired so easily.

'That sounds marvellous. But please, don't let me keep you from your work. I can find my own way.'

Mina selected a skewer of tropical fruit and settled further into her seat, taking her time. She wasn't going to jump to his bidding.

'And neglect you?' He shook his head and a lock of dark hair tumbled over his brow, making him look more like a beachcomber than a business tycoon.

Mina's gaze strayed towards his unbuttoned shirt and the display of taut, packed muscle. She tried not to stare but it became tougher by the second. Why didn't he do up his shirt? Did he think himself so sexy he had to flaunt himself? That she wouldn't be able to resist him?

The idea was laughable. Yet Mina admitted the sight of his powerful frame set tremors running deep inside her.

She'd seen plenty of men wearing less than he did. She'd drawn nudes, even sculpted them, yet this was different. *She* felt different as she slanted a look at all that unvarnished masculinity. Not like an artist with an eye for angle and perspective. But like a woman.

There was a curious buzz in her bloodstream and her breath seemed far too shallow. The feeling was somehow both enervating and exhilarating.

Mina met his remarkable eyes. Malachite or tourmaline? The green was as deep as a fathomless ocean and just as unreadable. Beautiful yet dangerous. Like ocean depths where an unwary diver might be lured to disaster.

Setting her jaw, she put down her food and stood up. She reminded herself she was pragmatic, not fanciful, despite her creative nature.

'I'd love a tour, if you have time.' Anything

was better than sitting, trying not to ogle a man she didn't even like.

The tour proved fascinating. More so than she'd anticipated. Alexei showed her the main rooms in his sprawling villa. Big, airy spaces that invited you to relax. And despite the presence of some stunning pieces of art that made Mina desperate to return for a longer study, the place didn't feel ostentatious, like a rich man's showpiece. It was luxurious but, above all, comfortable. Mina could imagine living here.

Nor did Alexei insist on a detailed tour of every designer detail. A wave of the arm indicated the cinema. Another incorporated his private wing. Then guest suites, gym and so on. As they passed outside, Alexei swept up two broad-brimmed hats and passed her one.

'It's easy to get sunburned.'

Mina didn't argue. She had a healthy respect for the power of the sun. In her country everyone covered up to shelter from its rays. Casting him a glance, she realised he looked more like a beachcomber than ever. An incredibly fit, sexy beachcomber who clearly didn't spend all his time lolling in a hammock with a cold beer.

They passed through a lush garden, with more sculptures she promised herself she'd come back to. Then they were out on a white sand beach, where small waves shushed ashore with the regularity of a heartbeat. There were no footprints on the sand. No other houses, only water and the birds in the trees and the warmth of the sun on her body.

It was paradise.

Mina dragged in a deep breath, rich with the tang of the sea, and sighed. How long had it been since she'd spent time away from crowds and cars? Not since her last visit to Jeirut. There she'd been rejuvenated by the rough majesty of the arid mountains, the sparkling clean air with its unique fragrance and the quality of the light that was unlike anything else.

'This is glorious.'

'I think so. There aren't many places like it.'

'With no neighbours?' She scanned the opposite end of the beach, seeing only the rise of a headland covered in a tangle of green forest.

'Partly that. But the island itself is pretty unique. It was never cleared for farming so a lot of the natural forest is left. Its conservation value is tremendous, especially for several species of endangered birds.'

Mina swung around to discover Alexei surveying her rather than their surroundings. She wasn't used to being the centre of attention, not since she'd given up her royal duties in Jeirut and disappeared into her life in Paris. Yet it wasn't just the fact Alexei watched her, it was the intensity of his regard. As if *he* were the artist and she a model.

'What are your plans for the island?'

'Plans?'

Mina turned back to the stretch of white sand, imagining it lined with buildings and an oversized marina. 'Ecotourism or some other sort of development?'

'You assume I'm going to develop it?' Something in his voice snagged her attention and she looked up at him. His gaze was shadowed by the brim of his hat and unreadable.

'You're a businessman. Anyone with commercial sense would see it has enormous money-making potential.'

'Is that what you see?' His voice dipped to a gravelly note that made her skin shiver.

Mina shook her head and tried to repress regret at the thought of it transformed into a busy holiday resort. 'I can see it, yes.'

'But you don't approve.' Had he read her so easily?

She shrugged. 'Not all progress is an improvement.' Her gaze took in the forest and a flash of bright colour as some small bird curvetted into the blue sky before disappearing again into the green.

'I agree.'

Mina started and swung back. 'You do?'

'Why so surprised? Even businessmen can appreciate beauty when they see it.'

Not all businessmen. Mina had met enough, so wrapped up in building more wealth or power, who never considered the impact of their actions on others or the environment.

At fifteen she'd had a stand-up argument with her father about a development proposal for the foothills near the capital. The scheme would bring short-term jobs but most profits would go offshore and the environmental damage would be catastrophic. In the end the plan was modified. It was one of the few times her father had been swayed. A local company had won the contract in a compromise between development and conservation. Now that area attracted tourists, drawn by the natural beauty and nearby facilities.

'Carissa?'

'Sorry.' She blinked and focused, reading the lines around his mouth that spoke of disapproval. 'What did you say?'

'I asked what you have against businessmen.'

'Nothing.' Just selfish rich guys who expected others to dance to their tune. Yet the vibe she got now from Alexei was a million miles away from that.

That intrigued her. Standing with the ocean lapping near their feet and Alexei's dark gaze heavy as a touch, Mina felt something new shiver through her. More than sexual awareness. More than impatience and indignation. Something that spread warmth and niggled at her protective, no, her combative attitude.

'So you're not going to change the place?' It seemed too good to be true.

'Oh, there'll be changes.' He waved his hand in an encompassing gesture.

Disappointment was sour on Mina's tongue. Why had she allowed herself to think otherwise? 'Such as?'

'Some cabins near the landing strip for visiting scientists and a small research facility.' Mina looked up and caught his fleeting smile. 'That's all.'

He'd deliberately led her on, and she'd fallen for it, because she was primed to believe the worst of him. And he'd guessed. Yet instead of taking offence, he was amused.

She hated to admit it but Alexei Katsaros threw her off balance. He was arrogant and annoying but he was perceptive and had a lighter, warmer side. Plus he valued this pristine environment as it was.

'Truly?'

'Truly. I spent my teens in a crowded city. Believe me, I realise how special this place is.' A slow smile curled his mouth and Mina felt the same curl etch a scrawl of heat deep inside. 'Now, how about I show you the spot where the turtles come in to lay their eggs?'

Silently Mina nodded. Then, following his example, took off her sandals, her feet sinking into fine, damp sand.

Because of Carissa, Mina and Alexei Katsaros were on opposing sides. When he discovered her deception he'd be livid. She couldn't afford to let her guard down. Yet spending time learning about him could only be to her advantage and Carissa's, couldn't it?

An inner voice warned Mina she was playing with fire. She should make an excuse and go back to her room.

But Mina had always been fascinated by fire and playing safe had never seemed so unappealing.

CHAPTER SIX

MINA'S HAND MOVED swiftly over the sketchpad, but her thoughts focused on the role she played. She should end this farce now.

She wouldn't betray Carissa and leave her prey to Alexei. Yet, with each hour, Mina grew more desperate. After two days on his island, the atmosphere grew thicker, more intense. He'd kept his distance physically but that only accentuated her catastrophic response to him.

As if it had a mind of its own, her body woke in his presence. The symptoms were depressingly irrefutable. Budding nipples, a surge of heat that threatened to flood her cheeks and flickered like wildfire in her veins. Butterflies the size of circling vultures in her stomach and a heavy, pulsing throb between her legs.

Sexual interest.

She could view it clinically. The trouble was that when they were together Mina felt anything but clinical detachment.

Frowning, she stared at her less-than-impressive sketch, then shoved it over the spiral spine of her drawing book to start afresh.

To make matters worse was Carissa's news, received via text. The elopement was delayed. Pierre was still in the USA, finishing negotiations on the tricky deal that he hoped would cement his professional success. Despite Carissa's pleas he was determined to stick it out, saying their future hinged on it. Mina sympathised. If his family disowned him for making a marriage they didn't approve, one of the pair needed a steady income. Carissa was talented but only starting her commercial design business.

Which meant Mina was stuck here for at least a couple more days, pretending to be someone else. Pretending to be impervious to Alexei. The strain was unbearable.

No other man had got under her skin like this. Just the mellow sound of his rare laugh or the deliberately confrontational twitch of one black eyebrow and her pulse revved out of control. Fortunately he never got close enough to touch. Despite those daydreams where he touched her in the most delicious, disturbing ways.

Mina set her chin and tried to focus on her drawing. She had work to do. An exhibition to prepare for. She couldn't sit in the Caribbean twiddling her thumbs. She needed...

Her hand stilled. There *was* a way out. Why hadn't she seen it?

Probably because her head was too skewed by thoughts of Alexei Katsaros.

Mina had accepted Carissa's assumption that her father's job would suffer if the marriage fell through. But surely it *must* fall through. Once Carissa was married to Pierre there'd be no question of a match with Alexei.

Besides, though Alexei could be daunting and demanding, the last couple of days had revealed another side to him. His manner with Marie and Henri indicated a man far more approachable and likeable than she'd imagined. A man who didn't expect to be treated as a superior being because he paid their wages. A man who could be surprisingly considerate.

He wasn't the complete ogre Carissa had imagined.

If Carissa, or, more accurately, Mina, were to say she couldn't go through with an arranged marriage, he'd have to respect that.

Mina blinked down at the half-formed sketch as she ran through the scenario in her mind. All she needed to do was say she'd considered but decided against the match. She'd be free to return to Paris, her work and her routine.

Funny how the thought didn't fill her with relief or anticipation.

Instead, Mina felt a pang of regret at the idea of leaving the island. And Alexei.

Her pencil dropped to roll unchecked across the paper. Mina blinked as it described a half circle on the page.

Was she serious?

Alexei Katsaros?

She huffed out a fierce breath. But it did no good to tell herself she didn't like big, bold, bossy men whose dark eyes twinkled with amusement just when she was about to explode with indignation.

Because she did. She liked him too much. Though he made her weak in ways she never wanted. For weakness was an invitation for men to trample you. She'd seen it too often.

'You look annoyed. Trouble with your drawing?' The deep voice came from beside her and Mina jumped. It was as if she'd conjured Alexei out of thin air by thinking of him.

She turned, her gaze on a level with snug faded jeans. Mina's heart rapped out a new, frantic tattoo as she fought not to let her eyes linger on the outline of muscled thighs. Instead she tilted her head up and up, till finally she met his quizzical gaze.

A jolt, like the impact of an electrical current, drove down through her body. Her breath stalled and the blood coursed faster in her veins.

This wasn't right. She didn't want to feel this or anything like it for Alexei. Despite his occasional charm he was the sort to stomp all over a woman.

'It's not going well.' She dragged her gaze back to the sketchpad and flipped it closed. The black cover mocked her with its blankness. That was how her brain was when he got near, and her artistic ability. How could she finish her designs when all she could concentrate on was him?

Suddenly it was imperative she put an end to this farce.

Mina was on her feet before she had time to think about it. 'I need to talk with you.'

Alexei stood so close her nostrils quivered at that delicious tang of citrus and cedar with base notes of warm male. Mina wanted to step away but he'd notice. He noticed everything.

'Of course.' He gestured to the chairs grouped on the wide veranda. 'Shall we sit?'

Mina was too agitated to sit. 'Let's walk.' Now

she'd decided on her course of action she wanted
it done. With luck, in a few hours she'd be on her
way to Paris. Fiercely she smothered a pang of
disappointment at the idea.

He wasn't good for her. No man who distracted
her this way could be.

'Of course.' He turned towards the path that led
to the beach. When they reached the fine sand
Mina tugged off Carissa's pink sandals and put
them to one side. Alexei, she noticed, was already barefoot. She liked the shape of his feet,
the strength and composition of bone, vein, heel
and arch.

The next time she sculpted a male nude she'd
search for a model with feet and hands like
Alexei. There was something powerful and appealing about them.

Catching her thoughts, Mina closed her eyes
in self-disgust.

'Carissa? What is it? Surely nothing too bad?'
For once there was no challenge or humour in
Alexei's tone. He sounded concerned. 'Are you
okay?'

'Absolutely.' She wiped her face of expression.
'But I need to tell you something.'

'I'm all ears.'

He began walking along the beach, heading

for the hard-packed sand near the water. Mina fell into step beside him, wondering how to proceed. In the end she decided a direct approach was best.

'I've been doing a lot of thinking, Alexei, and I can't marry you.'

For a heartbeat he said nothing. Then he turned his head to survey her, his easy stride never faltering.

'Can't? Is there some barrier I don't know about?'

Because, of course, it would never occur to him that she didn't *want* to marry him.

'I'm not ready for marriage. I'm just turning twenty-three.' Yet many of her peers in Jeirut were married with children.

'Whereas I'm past thirty.'

'It's not that.' As soon as she said it, Mina could have bitten her tongue. Predictably Alexei pounced on her comment.

'So what is it?' His tone was even, yet she fancied she caught something sharp behind the smooth cadence.

'It's not the right decision for me.' She should have known he'd probe. She should have taken time to get her excuse straight instead of grabbing the first opportunity to talk.

Alexei stopped and Mina was forced to halt. Reluctantly she turned and looked up at him. Behind his head, out to sea, dark storm clouds built, promising rain and relief from the sultry weather. For Mina, raised in a dry climate, the air felt heavy and close, almost claustrophobic. It made her edgy.

Or perhaps that was Alexei's sharp scrutiny. No trace now of the understanding, almost easygoing man she'd glimpsed lately.

'So it's not the age gap. What, then? The idea of having my children?'

Mina stood, mesmerised by the gleam in those stunning eyes. She felt something burgeon deep inside. Excitement. A well of tenderness as she imagined a toddler with black hair and green eyes, its expression morphing from serious to mischievous. Alexei's child. And hers.

Her heart dipped and a vast tremor shuddered through her.

It was preposterous. She'd known the man mere days. She had no plans for kids anytime soon.

Yet what she felt at that deep, visceral level couldn't be denied.

'No, you want children, don't you, Mina?' Alexei's voice was a soft thread, drawing through her, making her suddenly, shockingly aware that he was right.

Marriage had never been her goal. She hadn't played brides or pretended her dolls were babies. She'd only had one doll, a gift from a neighbouring monarch that was too precious to play with. She'd assumed she'd missed out on the so-called maternal instinct.

Yet with the right partner, Mina could imagine motherhood being wonderful.

With the right partner.

Suddenly Mina felt completely, devastatingly out of her depth. All these years she'd known herself and what she wanted—the right to choose, the chance to be an artist. She'd worked hard and that work was beginning to pay off. Now, out of nowhere, this man made her feel and want things she'd never wanted before.

He undermined her certainties and her understanding of herself. And he'd done it in mere days!

Her breath clogged in her chest and she looked away. 'It doesn't matter. I've considered this carefully and I can't marry you.'

Silence. So complete even the birds in the trees seemed to stop singing. All Mina heard was the soft shush of waves.

'You'll have to give me more than that.'

'Pardon?' She swung around and met his steady look. He didn't seem at all put out. Instead Alexei looked merely intrigued and perhaps…amused? No, that couldn't be.

'You'll have to give me a reason. Your father assured me you were interested. *You* led me to believe—'

'I led you to believe nothing!' *He* was the one who'd dragged her here. 'I'm telling you marriage is off the agenda.'

Relief buoyed her. How much easier to stand up to Alexei when he riled her than when he was likeable.

'I'm afraid I can't accept that. Not unless you give me a reason.'

'Can't accept?' Mina couldn't believe the gall of the man. Her hands found her hips and she gave him a laser stare that should have singed a few inches off his height but sadly seemed to have no impact on that oversized ego. 'Then how about this? I'm not attracted to you. If I'm going to play happy families with any man, I'd like there to be some chemistry between us.'

Her chest heaved and her chin tilted high as her gaze collided with his. Then he inclined his head and her breath came more easily. He'd got the message. See? It had been simple after all.

'I'll go and pack. I'm sure you'd rather—' Mina paused in the act of turning when a large hand wrapped around her arm.

'Not so fast, Princess.'

Alexei took in her startled expression, and the quick, convulsive swallow, the darted look at his hand on her arm—her warm, bare, silk-fleshed arm.

For two days he'd been careful not to touch her. Not even to brush against her, for his awareness of Carissa verged on the primal and he preferred to keep a cool head where the Carters were concerned. Especially as her father still proved elusive, despite the efforts of a top investigator to locate him.

Alexei breathed deep, scenting her, that tantalising aroma of exotic spice that made him want more. Far more than a single touch.

More than a provocative game of advance and retreat.

More than this brush-off.

The marriage arrangement was a sham, yet Carissa's dismissal rankled. Did she really believe she could simply turn her back on him?

'You want *chemistry*?' His voice hit a bass note and he felt her shiver. Her eyes widened and he caught a hint of vulnerability in that sherry-brown gaze. But then she lowered those long lashes, veiling her eyes before turning her head to survey his restraining hand. Her pointed stare and haughty expression were a silent demand that he release her.

Why silent? Because she didn't trust her voice? Alexei watched Carissa's pulse thrum at the base of her throat.

How could she say there was no chemistry when the air was charged with animal attraction?

He stepped close and still she didn't look up. Alexei frowned. She wasn't scared, was she? The bizarre thought hit out of nowhere, tangling his thoughts. It was contrary to everything he knew of her.

Carissa was proud, opinionated and brave, considering how most people bowed to his wishes. It wasn't as if she were inexperienced. Carter had mentioned a failed affair with a Frenchman.

No, it wasn't fear holding her still. He read the shallow rise and fall of her breasts, the rushing pulse.

'I can give you chemistry,' Alexei murmured. He put his hand beneath her chin and lifted it till she had no choice but to look at him. Her mouth was a mutinous line but her eyes… Her eyes glowed dark gold. Desire slammed into him.

She lifted a hand to his chest, pushing as she opened her lips, no doubt to protest. So Alexei stopped her with his mouth, muffling her words, drawing in her warm breath.

For a moment there was stillness as shock tore through him. Just this simple touch and he felt poised on the brink.

Then Alexei gave himself up to instinct and delved deep, cradling her head with one hand, shuffling his legs wider as he lashed his arm around her and fitted her in against him.

He'd known this would be good. How right he'd been.

She tasted like every desire made flesh, rich and tantalising. Different from any other woman yet somehow familiar. Alexei pressed harder, simultaneously demanding and coaxing a response till finally her tongue slipped against his, tentatively at first, almost shy.

This was unlike anything he could remember. A judder of pure need ripped through him. His hands tightened as she caressed him again, slowly, learning the taste and shape of his mouth. As if he were some new treat to be savoured.

That slow, cautious exploration was more arousing than anything he'd experienced in years. It was all he could do to stand there, letting her take her time, when every lick threatened to blow the back off his head. He shuddered and his groin tightened as if she'd reached out and taken his burgeoning erection in her hand rather than simply returned his kiss.

Alexei's breath expelled in a huff of satisfaction as her responses grew more voluptuous. Leaning in, he demanded more.

Their kiss became fervent. She trembled but there was nothing tentative about her caresses now. Her lips and tongue were bold and sensual, carnal and eager. Carissa had given up playing games. The honest hunger, the lack of pretence, fuelled Alexei's desire towards the point of no return.

At his chest her fingers dug into his shirt as if to stop him pulling back. He pushed closer, trying to assuage his body's demand for more. Carissa met him with demands of her own. Her slim body arched against him, her small, plump breasts thrusting up, her nipples hard and arousing as they scraped his torso.

A growl built at the back of Alexei's throat. A sound of satisfaction and need. She'd taken him from zero to a hundred in less time than a super-car on a circuit. His blood surged in his ears and his body clamoured for more.

Dropping both hands to her rump, he lifted her higher, inserting his thigh between hers. He was as taut and hot as newly worked metal. When she moved, rotating her hips, tilting her pelvis against him, Alexei wondered if he might shatter. His hands shook as he fought the impulse to strip her naked and take her here, on the sand.

Yet why hold back?

Despite that intriguing initial hesitation, Carissa was no innocent needing protection. Her kisses were the deep, drugging caresses of a woman ready for sex, and her body told its own story, of a highly sensual woman eager to mate.

He breathed deep through his nostrils, inhaling the scent of musk mingled with exotic spice and sea salt. There was no mistaking her arousal.

Alexei shuddered at what her undulating body did to his. He was more than hard. He was in pain. A pain that could only be assuaged by more, much more.

He lifted one hand, grazing it up her ribs to her breast, pulling back from her enough to close his hand over her.

Yes! Her breast filled his hand perfectly. Excitement flooded him as she arched further, thrusting herself into his palm. His erection throbbed against her softness and he heard her hiss of pleasure.

His qualms evaporated. Why wait? Why not?

Suddenly Alexei felt pressure on his chest. Two palms pushing at him. Carissa wriggling as if to get off his leg.

Her mouth broke from his and he heard her raw gasps. Still, he didn't relinquish his hold. He couldn't. His brain was locked onto the elemental need to mate. It wasn't what he'd intended when he kissed her but chemistry like this couldn't be ignored.

'No.'

At first the word didn't register as anything other than a sound. Then she said it again and he focused on her lips, red and slick from their kisses. Heat flooded his gut as he watched her mouth move and imagined her lips caressing his bare body.

He'd wanted Carissa before. From the moment she'd crossed his threshold and pretended to be unimpressed with him and his home. Her disdain had the perverse effect of sharpening his interest, especially when he had no trouble identifying the passion beneath it.

Now his need tested his control to the limit.

'Alexei, let me go!'

He frowned down into her beautiful face, seeing her mouth tighten, her jaw bunch, and her words filtered into his brain.

She couldn't be serious.

But she was. He caught what looked like desperation in the flicker of her eyes and immediately let her go. She stumbled back and he grabbed her by the elbows, holding her steady. She shook as if her legs wouldn't support her.

'Thank you.' Her eyes fixed on a point near his mouth and delicate colour washed her cheeks, highlighting her patrician features. Her hair had come undone, spilling a wash of dark silk across her shoulders. It had felt like gossamer in his hands. With the sun on it, it looked like some glossy, fabled treasure. Alexei wanted to catch it up in his hands.

He wanted to kiss her and feel again the triumphant moment when her yielding became a sensual demand.

Instead he released her and stepped back, disconcerted at the lingering strength of his desire. That was supposed to be a kiss to prove a point. Yet he felt he'd walked into an ambush. His gaze sharpened on Carissa but she looked just as poleaxed.

Yet as he watched, she regrouped. Her hands went to her hips and her chin rose. She drew a deep breath and Alexei's attention dropped to those proud, perfect breasts pouting against her pink T-shirt. His fingers twitched as he recalled the feel of her breasts. He wanted to discover if she tasted as good all over as her mouth did.

Inhaling sharply, Alexei took another step back and felt a rush of warm water around his bare feet as a tiny wave came ashore. He wished it were icy, and deep enough to wash away the erection still jutting against his jeans.

He wasn't in the habit of losing control. His mouth tightened.

'I'll go and pack.'

'Sorry?' He scowled down at her determined features.

Carissa made a vague gesture with one arm. 'I'd like to go home now.' Her gaze lifted briefly to his before skittering away again. 'If you can arrange the transport.'

Alexei shook his head, a harsh laugh grinding

from his throat. 'You've got to be kidding. You're not still pretending we're not attracted.'

'I…' She chewed her lip.

'Because if you are, maybe I should kiss you again. Then when we're naked on the sand and I'm deep inside you, you can tell me how sexually incompatible we are.' His voice dropped to a husky cadence as he imagined it. 'One more kiss is all it would take, Princess. You know it and I know it.'

Her nostrils flared and her eyes flashed. Alexei loved her passion. He wanted to reach out and touch it, bask in its heat.

'Nevertheless, I want to leave. I told you I won't marry you.'

Alexei shoved his hands into the pockets of his jeans as he surveyed his confusing guest. A woman who'd tampered with his peace since she arrived. Who'd distracted him more than was advisable when he still had to bring her father to book.

What game was she playing? Some elaborate sexual tease? Except it was clear she suffered as much as he from unfulfilled desire.

Impatience stormed through Alexei. At himself for being diverted. At Carter for not showing himself. At Carissa for making him feel like an out-of-control teenager instead of a mogul with the world at his feet.

'That's a shame, Princess. Because you're not going anywhere.'

CHAPTER SEVEN

MINA STARED UP into Alexei's set face—the haughty winged eyebrows, the set jaw, the calculation in those gem-bright eyes—and knew she'd blundered terribly.

How had she imagined leaving would be easy?

It would have been if you hadn't kissed him back. If you hadn't tried to climb onto him like some sex-starved nymphomaniac.

Her naivety was truly remarkable, she realised belatedly.

Not only was the attraction between them real, but Alexei was a man used to getting his way. Right now he wanted a bride. And since Mina had demonstrated how sexually compatible they were, he also wanted her, physically.

Excitement eddied deep inside at his possessiveness. It should annoy her. It *did*. And yet...

Heat flushed her throat and breasts as she recalled the weight of his erection. The way she'd ground herself against his thigh, trying to ease

ANNIE WEST 119

the desperate ache between her legs. The way one kiss had made her cast aside a lifetime's caution.

Maybe she was sex-starved after all. In twenty-two years she'd never felt anything like this compulsion. No man had come close to breaking her absorption in her art and arousing such fire.

'Don't call me Princess. I don't like it.'

Those expressive eyebrows lifted higher as if he were surprised she'd choose that to complain about. But the way Alexei said it in that deep, roughened voice cut too close to the real Mina.

In her youth she'd chafed at the title 'Princess,' for it encompassed all the restrictions placed on her life by her father and her birth. Yet it was indelibly, undeniably hers, something she could never erase, though she didn't use it.

Hearing it now, from this big bear of a man who smashed through all the layers of civilisation and control she'd built up over a lifetime, evoked an atavistic fear that he *knew* her as no one else did. That he recognised the real Mina. More, that the wild, reckless woman who'd lost her mind and her self-respect when he kissed her, *was* the real Mina.

Her jumbled thoughts were crazy, surely, yet she had to put at least an illusion of distance between them. Hearing him use her title, even if he didn't know how apt it was, made her feel he saw past her attempts to be indomitable.

Besides, the cynical way he said it made her shiver thinking of his retribution once he learned the truth.

'Then of course I won't call you that. Carissa.'

The name was a deliberate caress, the soft sibilant curling around her vital organs like a silken cord.

The terrible knowledge hit that Mina wanted to hear him say her real name like that. Not that it was nearly as musical. It was plain and ordinary, but the longing to hear it on his tongue was almost overpowering.

She folded her arms across her chest and stumbled back a step. He'd see that as proof of weakness but that wasn't as important as retaining her sanity.

What had he done to her?

How had a kiss tumbled her defences and addled her brain?

But it had been more than a kiss.

It had been momentous. Life-changing. Mina felt as if she'd woken from a dream to a new world where everything took on a sharp clarity. Where every sense was heightened and alert.

Where light and shadow were more defined, colour brighter, feelings more vivid.

She hefted a deep breath, saw his eyes flicker on the movement and angled her chin.

Weakened she might be, but she was no pushover.

'I'm sorry if my response just now misled you, Alexei.' She faced his stare head-on, telling herself this was nothing compared to challenges she'd faced as a royal. Except then she'd been confident in her own abilities. Now, suddenly, she realised she wasn't as strong as she'd believed. This man made her feel unexpectedly weak. 'But I'm serious. I don't want marriage.'

He folded his arms over his chest, the movement mirroring her posture. Yet on him the gesture was challenging rather than self-protective. She watched his biceps bulge and tried not to remember the iron-hard strength of his embrace. His virile power had been part of the magic she'd felt in his arms.

'So what do you want? An affair?'

'No!' Mina heard the shock in her voice and gave up any hope of pretending to be insouciant. 'My response was…a mistake.'

'A mistake?'

'You're a very persuasive kisser.' She refused

to look away, despite the heat warming her face. 'But I've decided I'm not ready to settle down and marry.'

Mina paused, waiting for him to respond but Alexei said nothing. 'I'm sorry to disappoint you. But it's better to know now than later.' She drew a slow breath, annoyance rising at his continued silence. 'In the circumstances I'd like to return to Paris.'

'That's not possible.'

'Not possible? Is there a problem with the plane?'

Alexei shook his head. 'I need you here until your father arrives.'

'Sorry?' Still dealing with shock at her physical response to Alexei, Mina found it hard to grasp his meaning.

'Have you heard from him recently?'

Mina frowned. 'Heard from him?'

'A phone call? Text or email?'

She shook her head.

That shadowy green gaze bored into her but now he didn't bother to hide his expression. It was sharp with disbelief. With distrust.

'It's true!' Mina had been thankful Carissa's father hadn't arrived, because it delayed the moment of her unmasking, giving her friend time to get away with Pierre. Now Mina's stomach sank and her skin tightened. She had a bad feeling that this situation was more complex and fraught than she'd suspected. What had she walked into?

'Then lend me your phone. I'll check the number I have for him. Clearly the one I've got is wrong. It's vital I contact him.'

Mina bit her lip. This conversation got odder and odder. But she could hardly refuse. 'I'll write it down for you.' She'd have to get it from Carissa.

'Hand over the phone, Carissa. That will do.'

There was something about the way he spoke, the air of ruthless command that sent warning cresting through her. Something was very wrong.

Drawing on years of royal training, she masked her tension. 'Of course. I'll go and get it now.'

She felt his suspicion like tiny pinpricks on her skin but eventually he inclined his head and relief juddered through her. For a moment she'd thought he'd insist on walking her back to her room.

Mina turned away, forcing herself not to run. But all the way to the house she felt shaky. From the sudden sense of foreboding when Carissa's father had been mentioned? Or from that kiss?

In her room she turned the latch to lock her

door and sagged against it, knees wobbly with reaction. But she had no time to waste.

Seconds later she had the phone in her hand, punching out Carissa's number. But her relief when her friend picked up was short-lived. Mina recognised the panic in Carissa's voice as she admitted she hadn't heard from her father. It wasn't like him to be out of contact so long. Worse, Pierre had rung again to confirm he wouldn't be back in Paris for two days. Could Mina hold out till then?

Mina pressed a hand to her forehead, her thoughts frantic. Two more days here wouldn't affect her work schedule too much. But did she really want to stay with Alexei Katsaros? Especially now the stakes seemed infinitely higher. What had started as a defiant plan to save her friend grew tangled and risky.

Then Carissa sniffed and said Mina should tell Alexei the truth. She'd done more than enough and it was time Carissa fought her own battles.

Mina was tempted to agree.

Except Carissa would be bulldozed by Alexei. She'd be cowed and if not browbeaten then emotionally blackmailed into doing what her father and Alexei wanted. Could Mina stand by and see that happen to her dear friend?

There was even a part of her that protested at the idea of Alexei with Carissa, not for Carissa's sake but Mina's.

Where had that come from?

Mina drew a steadying breath and thrust aside the wayward thought. She warned Carissa to move out of her apartment as a precaution, in case the masquerade came unstuck and Alexei came looking for her.

Then she ended the call and stared at the phone in her hand. If she was to play this role any longer she couldn't let Alexei see her call history or contacts. It would be obvious she wasn't Carissa.

Which meant refusing to hand over her phone.

Adrenalin rushed her bloodstream at the thought of Alexei discovering the truth. But there was no other option.

All she had to do was hold out for a couple more days.

A rap on her door made her stiffen.

'Carissa?'

Mina's heart thumped and she knew a craven desire to admit defeat. To open the door and tell him everything.

Except Carissa relied on her. Carissa, who'd been there when Mina was desperately homesick and convinced she'd never make it as an artist.

Carissa, whose warm, gentle nature made her the best friend Mina had ever had. The only real friend, since all the people she'd mixed with in Jeirut had been hand-picked by her father.

Carissa didn't care about her royal status. She liked Mina for herself. She was genuine and caring and Mina refused to see her throw her happiness away for some moody tycoon.

Mina breathed deep and tiptoed to the glass door that led outside.

Behind her the door rattled. 'Carissa?'

The sound sent her catapulting into the garden, eyes on the path to the beach, her phone gripped in one clammy hand.

He wouldn't be happy. In fact, Alexei would be furious. The thought lent her speed, though of course there was no real escape. The best she could do was ensure he didn't discover she wasn't Carissa. It still amazed her that he hadn't bothered to check her photo. No one but the immigration official had bothered to view her passport.

Her stride slowed as she approached the beach. Did she really mean to—

A rhythmic thudding reached her ears. Louder than her pumping heart. Mina looked over her shoulder and saw Alexei covering the ground between them in long strides. For a second, a primitive thrill of fear engulfed her, freezing her limbs. But Mina was no cornered prey. Her hand tightened on the phone. Then she turned, hauling her arm back and letting go.

Alexei grabbed her arm a moment too late. She heard his rough breathing, felt the clamp of his fingers on her wrist and the heat of his massive frame behind her as the phone arced over the water and disappeared into the endless azure sea.

The die was cast.

With a sense of disbelief, Alexei watched the phone plummet into the sea.

He'd almost convinced himself that despite her contrariness Carissa was an innocent pawn in her father's scheme.

Because her kiss blew you away.

A kiss meant nothing. Logically he knew that, yet Alexei had been close to believing in her.

Because he'd wanted her since she stepped across his threshold. Her feisty attitude and subtle sexiness were a unique turn-on, especially combined with that indefinable sense of connection, as if behind the charades they played he knew her and she him. As if at a level so deep it defied logic, they understood each other.

When they'd kissed it was combustible. *He'd* been combustible.

She'd been far more than he expected. Responsive. Blatantly hungry for him, wildly passionate and yet, when he'd first tasted her he'd sensed a hesitance that felt almost like innocence.

Innocence! She was in cahoots with her thieving father. She was messing with his mind.

'You're so desperate that I don't contact your father?' He slid his free arm around her waist, holding her back against him in a travesty of the passionate embrace they'd shared on this very beach.

Now the passions he felt were fury and jarring disappointment. He'd actually wanted to believe in Carissa.

Because you want her in your bed. You'd begun to trust her. Even now, knowing she's part of his scam, you can't turn off your hunger.

It was true. His arm around her middle wasn't lover-like and his grip on her wrist was unbreakable, yet his body reacted to the soft pressure of her rump against him, the underside of her breasts brushing his arm and the scent of her hair teasing his nostrils.

If anything, ire hiked his arousal higher. His sharpened senses picked up her ragged breathing and her quick, thrumming pulse and the tension of her muscles, as if she waited for him to slacken his hold so she could run.

There was nowhere she could go that he wouldn't find her.

Suddenly, their situation took on a whole new, delectable piquancy.

'I didn't want you prying into my private messages.' Her voice was choppy, and Alexei felt as well as heard her harsh breathing.

'Why's that, Carissa? Have you been sexting with your French boyfriend?'

Her hissed breath confirmed it. Alexei's constraining arm tightened. At the idea of her sharing erotic messages and images with another man?

Impossible.

Yet he felt a deep satisfaction that while she was on his island she'd have to devote all her attention to him. There'd be no other men in her life.

'You know about him?' Her voice was wary.

'Was he supposed to be a secret?' Of course he was. She'd even faked a show of tremulous innocence when her lips met his. Not that it had lasted.

'My messages are my affair. You have no right to pry. You're a bully.'

She yanked her arm, trying to free it. The movement was so violent it slammed her into even more intimate contact with Alexei's hardening body. Flame shot through him as she rubbed against his groin.

Carissa froze, her breath a shocked hiss. He felt the pulse at her wrist sprint out of control as if she only now realised how intimately close they stood.

'You think I care about seeing your nude photos? All I want is to bring your father out of hiding.'

'Hiding? What are you talking about?'

Alexei applauded her acting skills. She sounded confused rather than guilty. 'Spare me the dramatics. Only a woman desperate to hide the truth would pitch her phone. You're in this with your father.' He hadn't quite believed she'd do it, even as she drew her arm back in that perfect curve. 'You've just proved it.'

She was silent for so long he wondered if she were about to admit defeat till she said in a completely different tone, 'In what?'

Furious and sick of her lies, he spun her round, his hands on her narrow waist.

Yet, reading her expression, Alexei felt a splinter of doubt.

'What has he done?' Instead of avoiding his stare, she peered up at him, a tiny wrinkle between her eyebrows, her look searching.

Probably hoping to pretend that she didn't know.

'Embezzled a fortune. And that's just the funds he's stolen in the last couple of months. Who knows what the total is in the years he's worked for me?' Alexei spoke through clamped teeth, watching her eyes grow wide.

He'd thought his financial systems the best. The rigorous accounting and auditing processes were held up as the gold standard. But when the man who designed them was the one with his fingers in the till...

'You're sure?' Carissa looked the picture of shock. He felt a tremor pass through her and held her more firmly, telling himself he didn't want her pretending to faint. It wasn't dramatics he wanted but retribution.

'Absolutely. There's a complete audit underway. You can be sure it will uncover every cent he's stolen. Including the money that's supported your party lifestyle while you pretend to be an artist.'

The fact some of the stolen money had funded

this woman's taste for idle self-gratification twisted the knife. Alexei had laboured hard for everything he possessed. It had been tough, especially scraping together capital to invest in his first innovative software package when he'd had no track record and only a mediocre education. He hadn't even had a permanent roof over his head.

Nothing had been handed to him. And he knew all about leeches who fattened themselves by living off the hard work of others.

Yet he'd allowed himself to be conned by Carter.

He stared down into soft brown eyes and knew they lied. His voice held bitter amusement. 'After this you'll have to work for a living like the rest of us. That will be a novel experience for you.'

Now Mina understood the rage flaring in that deep green gaze, the snap of his words and the harsh jut of his chin. It was like staring into the boiling heart of a volcano.

The raw quality of his emotion should unnerve her. Yet at the same time, that elemental ferocity drew her.

Was she mad?

Her father had always said she was reckless,

yet there was something so vital about Alexei in this moment. Even as she warned herself to be careful, her artist's eye was busy cataloguing the changes in him, the way potent masculine anger imbued every sharp angle and bunched muscle.

Already his hold on her waist loosened. Was she ridiculously naive? Yet the vibe she picked up from Alexei was the same as she got from her brother-in-law, Huseyn. When he'd first appeared, Huseyn had been the enemy, storming in to snatch the kingdom and her sister in marriage. Big, abrupt and deliberately provoking, he'd nevertheless proved appearances wrong. He'd turned out to be a devoted family man and an unobtrusively kind brother-in-law, whose bark was worse than his bite, at least with those he cared for.

Was Alexei like him? Or did her instinct lie because she was attracted? And because she battled a compulsion to commit that sparking, urgent energy to paper? Mina wanted to capture his aura of power.

Almost as much as she wanted that energy focused on kissing her again.

She blinked. She couldn't take her safety for granted.

'Do you plan to hurt me because of him?' Mina

had no idea if confronting Alexei directly was the right approach but she had to know.

His head reared back, a scowl settling on his forehead. 'I suppose you'll find it tough to work for a living instead of living off your father's ill-gotten gains. But I'd hardly call that hurting.'

'I mean, are you so angry you'll *hurt* me.'

She saw the moment her meaning registered. Alexei's instinctive recoil and the horror in his eyes.

His hands dropped to his sides. 'No! Of course not.'

'There's no *of course*. Some men do.'

Slowly he inclined his head, his breath expelling in a rush of warm air that feathered her hair. 'Not me. Not ever.'

Mina surveyed him steadily, wondering whether to believe him, and her instinct.

'I think you're wrong about the theft. I think it's a mistake. Maybe someone else stole the money and made it look like he did it.' What she knew of Carissa's father pointed to an honest man, though his idea of engineering an arranged marriage was bizarre. Maybe his recent bereavement had affected him more than Carissa feared.

Alexei shook his head. 'There's no doubt. It

was definitely him.' He raised his eyebrows as if challenging her to prove otherwise.

'Well, if so, he didn't fritter it away funding parties in Paris.' Carissa's father had paid his daughter's art school tuition and now helped with part of her rent, but Carissa was talented and hardworking, supplementing her income from her art by waitressing and modelling. Even her shopping addiction for second-hand clothes was a source of income since she sold items she'd refurbished.

Alexei merely crossed his arms over his chest. He looked as unmoved and unmovable as the rocky outcrop at the far end of the beach.

Mina suppressed a sigh. What was the point of protesting Carissa's blamelessness? He'd never believe her. And, if he'd been ripped off so badly, who could blame him?

She slicked her tongue around her parched lips, feeling the rush of her pulse and the jitter of nerves still unsteady after that sprint to the beach, with Alexei at her heels. And Alexei holding her against him as if he'd never release her.

In fury, Mina reminded herself. Not desire. She was the one plagued by that. To Alexei she was a conniving thief, or as good as.

She shivered and looked away, out over the

water where the dark clouds grew more threatening by the moment. The humid air felt heavy, sultry with ominous foreboding.

It was hard not to see it as a sign, a warning that Alexei had some revenge planned.

Of course! Abruptly she swung towards him. His gaze was already on her, sending sensation wrinkling down her backbone. Mina's mouth tightened. She had to stop *reacting* to him!

'Why am I here, Alexei? What do you really want?'

'Don't look so worried. Nothing's going to happen to you that you don't want.'

Mina took a second to digest that. It should have reassured except the dark speculation in his eyes and her answering tremor of awareness undermined certainty. As if their bodies spoke a different language. As if he expected her to *want* far more than was good for her.

Mina refused to go there. Bad enough to find her first stirrings of real desire were for a man who didn't trust or like her. Who was, to all intents and purposes, her enemy.

She crossed her arms, mirroring his posture. 'Why am I here, Alexei? And don't give me that line about wanting to marry. That's clearly a lie.'

One dark eyebrow slanted. 'You take offence at a lie?'

Mina was about to tell him she abhorred dishonesty as much as she did selfish men who manipulated women for their own ends. Then she remembered she was here under false pretences. For the best of reasons, but still...

'Spit it out, Alexei.'

His eyes held hers. 'You're bait, to draw your father out. Since he had the front to suggest I marry you, I figure when he learns you're here, he'll assume his theft hasn't been discovered or that I'm willing to come to some agreement with my soon-to-be father-in-law.' His disdainful tone and chilly stare told her how likely that was.

'And until he gets here?' She swallowed. Her throat was tight and she had a hard time projecting calm.

'Till then you're my trump card.' His lips curved in a smile she could only describe as dangerous. 'I'll keep you close.'

CHAPTER EIGHT

THE SOUND OF the wind finally distracted Mina. She looked up from the intricate design taking shape on her sketchpad and realised the noise she'd been vaguely aware of was the howl of a strong wind from the sea. The dark clouds had moved closer in the hours since her confrontation with Alexei and the light was lurid green.

The hairs on Mina's nape and arms lifted. She didn't know tropical weather, but that eerie light reminded her of the explosive storms that occasionally devastated the mountains of her homeland.

A crash made her jump. Mina put her drawing down and crossed to her bedroom window.

A sun umbrella had fallen, knocking over a wrought-iron chair. As she watched, a cushion tumbled past and came to rest against a gardenia hedge.

Mina opened the door and went out, feeling the whip of the wind. Another cushion floated in the pool. She concentrated on saving the rest, gathering them and dropping them inside her room.

As she turned around, a chair slid, screeching across the flagstones. Mina chewed her lip, looking beyond the garden to the taller trees, bending in the wind. If the storm worsened, unsecured furniture could be dangerous, especially in a house with so many big windows. As for that umbrella…

She was grappling with it, trying to close it against the force of the wind when she heard a voice behind her.

'Leave that to me.' Large hands took over, Alexei's shoulder nudging her out of the way. She watched the strain of bunching muscles and tendons in his arms as he fought to close it, then heard a grunt of satisfaction as he finally succeeded. 'You get inside. This will get worse before it gets better.' He was already lifting the long umbrella pole and marching away.

Mina frowned, staring as he disappeared around the corner of the house. What had she expected? Thanks for trying to help? She should have known better.

But as another chair careered across flagstones, she set her mouth, grabbed it and followed him.

Nearby, yet screened from the house, was a

large garage. Inside, in addition to the four-wheel drive, she discovered a couple of jet skis, a wind-surfer, canoes and Alexei, stacking the furled umbrella against a pile of outdoor furniture. He must have been working for some time, secur-ing it all. Mina had been so busy working she hadn't noticed.

'Where's Henri?'

Alexei's head jerked up. He hadn't heard her approach over the noise of the wind. 'Gone with Marie to the larger island for supplies. But the storm's changed course, coming in faster than expected. They'll have to stay there till it blows over.'

Even in the gloom Mina could see the gleam of Alexei's steady stare. Did he expect her to panic at the idea of a powerful storm?

'What can I do?'

'Sorry?'

Behind her the door banged shut, leaving them in almost darkness. But not completely. Mina could make out his towering form, close now. The wide spread of his shoulders, the jut of his jaw as if he were still furious.

Mina didn't step back. To retreat would be to admit fear. She might be stuck here, an unwill-ing guest of an angry host who saw her as an avaricious plotter, but she refused to show anxiety. Even if there *was* something about Alexei Katsaros that made her breathing ragged and her pulse skip.

But it's not fear, is it?
It's desire.

Mina inhaled a breath redolent with the tang of citrus and Alexei, and strove to ignore the flurry in her belly.

'You said the storm's coming more quickly than expected and Henri's not here to help. What can I do to prepare?'

Alexei peered down at the slim figure before him, wishing it were light enough to read her expression.

It wasn't the first time she'd surprised him. When he'd rounded the house to find her struggling with the oversized umbrella his heart had almost stopped. Did she have any idea how dangerous that would have been, if the wind had ripped it out of her hold? How much damage it could do as a projectile?

'Get into the house and stay there.' He had enough to do without worrying for her safety. The wind was still rising.

For answer, she spun on her foot, headed for

the door and yanked it open. Alexei saw her silhouetted against the light, long legs, short white shorts and a tight top that outlined a deliciously willowy body. He remembered the feel of her against him; the combination of taut flesh and enticing, feminine softness had been irresistible.

Then she strode towards the house.

Good riddance. Alexei had more to do and time was running out. Yet, as he carted more furniture to the garage, he found Mina marching towards him, carrying another chair. The wind had strengthened and her long dark hair whipped around her face.

'What are you doing? Get inside. Now!'

For answer she kept walking, would have passed him if he hadn't caught her arm.

Her haughty stare could have stripped bark from a tree. 'There isn't time to argue. Accept my help and do what you have to. What about shutters? I can't see any. How do we protect the windows?'

Alexei paused, surprised to discover she was serious. She planned to help him batten down for the storm. 'They're electric. They'll come down at the punch of a button.'

'Then shouldn't you go and punch that button before we lose power?'

She was right. Plus he wanted to double-check the backup generator.

Alexei considered picking her up bodily and carrying her inside. She'd be safe. But no doubt she'd race back out here as soon as his back was turned.

'Very well.' He cast a look at the trees bending in the wind and, behind them, the inky, threatening sky. 'But only five minutes more. The main entrance will be open. Come in that way.' He lowered his head to her level, watching her pupils dilate. 'No longer than five minutes. Got it?'

Silently she nodded.

But when the time was up, Carissa was nowhere to be seen. The wind was stronger now, the sound like a freight train approaching from a distance. They had to take shelter. They didn't have much time left. Fat drops of rain fell and a second later he faced a grey sheet of solid water.

His mouth tightened as he scanned the exterior of the house. All the furniture was shut away. The house was secure, storm shutters in place. But Carissa was nowhere to be found.

Alexei called her name but the wind tore the sound away. Anxiety nipping at him, he sped through the garden, drenched by the needling deluge.

He couldn't see her. Not near the pool or house. He ventured further into the garden, blinking to clear his vision. With each passing second tension coiled tighter, his pulse racing faster.

Alexei rounded a curve in a path to see something staggering towards him. The sight was so unexpected, the shape lurching drunkenly, that it took precious seconds to process what he saw. When he did, he stifled an oath and raced forward, anger vying with stupefaction.

A sculpture! She'd stayed out in *this* to save a sculpture.

Arms out, he grabbed the ungainly wooden shape as Carissa staggered against him, blown by the force of the gale.

'Leave it! It's not worth it.' He felt her flinch. Saw her eyes widen as he tugged it from her.

She clung on like a limpet, mouthing something he couldn't hear. 'Save...together.'

Alexei shook his head. 'Inside. Now!'

Whether she heard him over the wind's rising scream, Alexei didn't know. But her mouth set in a mulish line as she held on tight. They didn't have time to argue. The wind was still picking up speed. Soon the flying debris would be larger, more dangerous.

Hefting the sculpture more securely, Alexei grabbed her hand and started back down the path.

The way back took forever. The sodden ground was treacherous and the wind buffeted mercilessly. More than once he saved Carissa from falling when her foot skidded. Then, as they approached the house, the wind caught Alexei and the wildly rotating sculpture full force and almost plunged them into the pool. He would have dropped it there and then, except this time Carissa was dragging at his arm, holding him steady.

Cursing, Alexei regained his balance and lurched forward. His muscles strained at the effort of carrying the cumbersome sculpture that wanted to fly from his arms into the screeching wind.

Darkness. The slam of the door. Stillness after that riot of rushing air and hammering rain.

Alexei struggled to the control panel on the wall, jamming his elbow against the switch that brought down the final storm shutter. Another jab and light filled the foyer.

His breath came in rough gasps that tore his throat. Water sluiced down his face and he almost lost balance in the spreading pool of water as he bent to lower his ungainly burden.

Finally he straightened to stare at the convoluted collection of carved sails that still spun and shivered with the dying momentum of the wind. No wonder it had felt as if it might take off from his arms. It was designed to move in a breeze. Breeze, not a cyclone!

Alexei had bought it as a brilliant, evocative piece that paid homage to the centuries of seafarers who'd passed this way. Now, looking past the still-turning sails to the woman beyond, he wished he'd never seen it.

She could have been hurt. More than hurt.

The savage clench of his ribs around his organs wrapped fiery pain around Alexei's torso.

Mina was bent forward, hands on knees, dragging in desperate, gasping breaths. Her hair was a slick, dark curve that arrowed over her shoulder. Her nipples stood proud against the dark cherry pink of the top that plastered her breasts. Her slim legs glistened with water and there was a long red scratch on her shin.

'What. The. Hell. Were. You. Thinking?' He ground the words out.

Her eyes lifted. A second later Carissa straightened, abandoning her recuperative pose for that now-familiar haughty stance. Chin forward, slender neck stretched high, eyebrows slightly raised. She did obstinate condescension to perfection.

'Saving a wonderful work of art.' She reached into a back pocket of her shorts and produced a large screwdriver. That explained how she'd dislodged the sculpture from its plinth. She must have grabbed it from the garage.

'What on earth possessed you?'

Still not quite believing what she'd done, he watched as she turned away and put the screwdriver down on a side table. It landed with a clatter. There was a jagged tear at the hem of her T-shirt and another scratch down the back of one toned thigh.

Alexei felt something surge high inside. Something rough and sharp, scrabbling and clawing at his control. He clenched his jaw so tight he wondered if he'd ever unlock it.

A spasm shook him as he remembered the waving boughs, the lashing storm and thought of the lucky escape she'd had.

Carissa turned, eyes dark and wide in her too-pale face. 'We couldn't leave it there. It's a masterpiece.'

Alexei stared. He couldn't believe what he heard.

'You know it is.' Her voice was clipped. 'Otherwise you wouldn't have bought it.'

He knew all right. He wouldn't have paid the exorbitant amount he had for it otherwise. But that didn't matter.

'That was the single most stupid, irresponsible thing I've witnessed in years.' His voice lashed as he relived the sight of her, refusing to budge without her precious sculpture. 'I don't care about the money.'

She flinched, her face paling even more. 'Of course you don't! Obviously I was mistaken. You probably bought it because it had a big price tag to match your big ego.' She drew a breath that emphasised how shaky she was, despite her show of defiance. She looked proud and glorious and frighteningly vulnerable. And Alexei couldn't understand why the vein of fury ran so deep and strong within him.

It was a good thing they were on opposite sides of the room. Dimly he realised fear fed his anger. That terrible moment when he'd discovered her missing. Guilt that she could have died out there because he hadn't forced her inside earlier.

'It's not worth your life. Do you have any idea how dangerous it was out there?' Alexei heard his voice rise from a hoarse whisper to something close to a roar. 'Are you really that thoughtless? That unbelievably stupid?'

His loss of control stunned him. When had he ever been this angry? When he'd discovered her father's theft he'd been livid, determined to get justice. He'd felt personally betrayed, made a fool of by the one person he'd trusted in years. But he hadn't experienced this visceral level of dismay. This gut-scouring scrape of horror.

Carissa didn't flinch. She faced him with cool—almost *too* cool—composure.

Finally the echo of his words died. Outside the wind wailed, but in here there was nothing but the sound of heavy, uneven breaths and the tumble of rushing blood in his ears.

'If you'll excuse me, I have a cut I need to attend to, before I stain your floor.'

Carissa spun around and walked away down the dark corridor towards her suite. Belatedly he realised she was cradling one hand. And that she walked with the careful precision of someone marshalling their strength to stay upright.

The red mist edging Alexei's vision began to clear. The cyclonic rage eased. His brain kicked into gear, enough to suspect her superior bearing hid something other than disgust at his fury.

His gaze dropped to the floor. A spatter of dark

droplets led down the corridor. The sight was a kick to the belly.

Her hand was bleeding and he hadn't noticed. He'd been too busy berating her.

Alexei slumped against the wall, palming his wet face, trying to scrub away the last vestiges of blinding fury.

He still reeled from the fact Carissa had pitched in to help secure the house, making herself useful as if she wasn't the spoiled, self-absorbed woman he'd pegged her as. Alexei had expected her to demand he spirit her off the island. Or that she'd cower in the house, frightened by the ferocity of the weather. He wouldn't have blamed her.

Carissa never did what he expected. *She* wasn't what he expected.

Now she made him feel as if *he* were in the wrong.

Residual anger made his heart pound his ribcage. Yet that didn't explain the unfamiliar, queasy feeling in his belly. It wasn't fear, not now she was safe.

Surely it wasn't guilt? She *had* risked her neck out there.

The woman was trouble.

Alexei straightened from the wall, circled around the sculpture that had caused this drama, and headed towards the light streaming from her suite. He needed to see how badly she was hurt.

Mina bit her lip and tried to stop shaking enough to tear open the box of sticking plasters she'd found in the bathroom. It dropped to the floor and she sagged against the wall, eyes closing.

She'd pick it up in a minute, when the shaking stopped.

She was so angry. But soon she'd be calm.

Except it wasn't simply anger that made her tremble from head to foot. Mina wiped her un-injured hand across her cheeks, scrubbing away the fresh trails of wetness that had nothing to do with the sodden hair dripping down her face.

There was a blockage in her throat, hot and sour, making it hard to swallow. A ball of emotion that refused to go away.

Stupid. Thoughtless.

The words circled again and again. She didn't know how to silence them.

Mina told herself she was in shock. The storm had been terrifying. When she'd started out to save the sculpture, the wind hadn't been so bad and she'd been sure she'd have time. Then all hell had broken loose and she'd been stunned to realise danger was upon her, upon *them*. It was her fault Alexei had been out there too.

What if he'd been hurt trying to save her?

Her mouth crumpled and a sob seared her clogged throat.

Mina shook her head. She didn't cry. She never cried. Not even when her father died.

Stupid. Thoughtless.

She swallowed again and this time tasted tears.

The last time she'd seen her father they'd argued. She'd wanted to go to art school and he'd already enrolled her in university to major in economics. It was one of the rare times he'd lost his temper. Usually he was cool and distant. He expected his daughters to obey, to do whatever he expected, including acquiring appropriate qualifications to prove women in Jeirut could play a part in the country's modernisation.

There was no room for an artist in the royal family. Mina's value, like her sister Ghizlan's, lay in being *useful*.

Their father's focus was the country, not them. He'd never cuddled them or laughed with them. Never been close, let alone shown love. They were tools in his grand plans. Her mother had died when she was an infant so there was no one to argue on her behalf.

But at seventeen, Mina had believed she had a right to choose her career. Her father had put paid to that. He'd been brutally frank about her purpose in life. As a princess she'd be a model for Jeiruti women and have a key role in royal events. In time, she'd make a dynastic marriage to a man her father chose.

Mina was stupid, thoughtless and selfish to question his plans.

Two days later he'd dropped dead from a brain aneurism.

She'd never had a chance to mend the breach between them. She told herself it didn't matter because her father hadn't loved her, or she him. Yet regret lingered. Hearing those words again, whiplash sharp—

'Carissa? Are you all right?'

Mina's eyes popped open, horror enveloping her. She caught sight of herself in the mirror and groaned. Her eyes were pink and she couldn't stop her mouth quivering.

'Yes.'

The door rattled. 'Why have you locked the door?'

Mina sank her teeth into her bottom lip. She didn't need this. She didn't have the energy to face Alexei. She needed time to marshal her defences.

'Carissa?'

'I want privacy. Is that too much to ask?' Her shaking grew worse, not better. She wrapped her arms around herself, trying to hold in the ache. And the cold. She felt so cold.

'Open the door, Carissa. I need to make sure you're okay.'

Great. Another man who refused to take a woman's word or believe she could look after herself.

But Alexei thought her stupid, didn't he?

To her horror, fresh tears prickled her eyes and she blinked frantically. She felt...raw, unprotected, unable to summon the assurance she projected to keep people at a distance.

It was ridiculous. Words couldn't hurt her. Yet Alexei's expression as he'd spoken... The knowledge he'd been right—

'Open the door *now*, Carissa, or I'll break it down.'

'I said—'

'Now!' He didn't shout like before. But the low resonance of his voice convinced her more than any ranting threat.

Mina stumbled to the door and flicked the

latch. It swung open and Alexei surged in, making her back up.

She refused to meet his eyes, turning instead to the packet she'd dropped on the floor. 'Since you're here—' she tugged in a swift breath and tried to sound nonchalant '—would you mind picking that up? My hands are a bit unsteady.' There was no way of hiding that so she might as well admit it.

Without waiting for a response Mina turned to the basin and ran water over the jagged cut in the fleshy part of her hand, cleaning away the dripping blood. Her grasp of the screwdriver had slipped on the last screw and dug into her flesh. Strange, she couldn't feel any pain.

'Here, let me.' A large hand took her elbow and Alexei pushed her down onto a chair beside the vast bath. His touch was surprisingly gentle. Mina opened her mouth to protest but found she didn't have the inclination. Her shoulders slumped as her energy ebbed.

Alexei wrapped a fluffy white hand towel around her hand. Mina frowned, thinking of blood on the pristine cloth, but said nothing. It was his towel.

He took her other hand and pressed it to the cloth to keep the pressure steady. Then he collected the packet she'd dropped plus a bottle from the cupboard and hunkered before her.

She was aware of his heat above all, like a furnace sending out warmth to tease her frozen body. But she refused to meet his eyes. Instead she concentrated on those hard, beautiful hands. They worked deftly.

'This will sting.' He unwrapped the towel and dabbed the wound. Mina felt the burn of antiseptic but didn't flinch.

'It doesn't look too deep.'

'No. Fortunately it drove along my hand instead of in.' If it had surely she wouldn't feel so calm. A major injury to her hand would be catastrophe.

Alexei's grip tightened for a second, then eased. Mina frowned, watching him work. A moment later it was all over.

'How does that feel?'

'Fine.' She flexed her hand, discovering she'd stopped shaking as he held her. 'Thank you.'

He didn't move. Beyond the thick shutters, Mina heard the rush of the wind driving against the building. It reminded her of the danger she'd put them both in.

Her heart thudded against her ribs as if trying to fly away on the storm. She drew in another breath, this time through her mouth, trying not to inhale Alexei's spicy scent. The storm seemed to have heightened it rather than washed it away.

'Carissa, I'm sorry. I—'

Mina surged up, stepping sideways, away from him. It felt wrong, hearing him apologise, when she'd been at fault.

It felt even more wrong, hearing him call her by someone else's name. She wanted *her* name on his lips. How crazy was that?

'No. Don't.' She swallowed. He rose and she fixed her eyes on his collarbone. 'I apologise. I was wrong to put you in danger by making you look for me.' She sucked in a shallow breath. 'You're right. A sculpture isn't as important as a person.' If he'd died because of her...

Reluctantly she lifted her eyes and met his deep green gaze. A thrill of recognition and awareness shot down her spine. Strangely, he didn't look angry any more.

'It *was* stupid of me. I thought I had more time. Obviously I underestimated the force and speed of the storm.'

'I applaud your desire to save the sculpture. Just not your timing.' His mouth flattened. 'I shouldn't have spoken the way I did. That was fear talking. But it was no excuse.'

'You were frightened?' Alexei had seemed so in control, so competent, it hadn't entered her mind he was frightened.

'I was frantic. You could have been badly hurt.'

His eyes locked on hers and Mina felt as if she were being pulled under by a jade-green sea, sucked into an undertow where, no matter how she struggled, she couldn't break free.

Or had she forgotten to struggle? She tried to rouse herself from this strange torpor but couldn't.

'I'm tougher than I look.'

Alexei inclined his head. 'So I'm learning. It took guts to do what you did.' His words astounded her.

'And stupidity.' She couldn't let it go.

Something shifted in his expression. 'You thought it important. That made it courageous.'

His words sowed a kernel of heat deep inside. Heat that glowed and spread as he stared down at her.

'Does that mean you don't despise me quite as much as before?' Better to remind them both that they were on opposing sides than be lulled into surrendering her guard any further.

'I don't despise you.' Alexei's voice was gruff as he lifted his hand to wipe the tear tracks from her cheeks. His touch ignited a terrible yearning. Mina had to fight to not lean closer.

'I find that hard to believe.' Mina moved back, breaking contact, injecting hauteur into her expression.

Alexei followed, hemming her in and planting a palm on the wall beside her head. 'You infuriate me. Intrigue me.' His voice dropped to a low note that resonated through her. 'Attract me.'

Mina's pulse thundered as she read the stark determination in his eyes. She struggled to hang on to anger but it slipped like precious water from her hands.

'That's impossible.' It had to be. Because she feared she didn't have the strength to remember they were enemies.

'Then perhaps you'll believe this.' Alexei leaned in and every emotion, every sensation Mina had tried not to feel, exploded into life.

CHAPTER NINE

THE TOUCH OF his lips on hers was gentle yet not tentative. As if he gave her time to adjust to the inevitable.

And it *did* feel inevitable.

As if she'd waited half her life for this. As if the kiss they'd shared on the sand hours ago had evoked a longing that, once roused, couldn't be assuaged or argued away by common sense.

Common sense?

Where was that as Mina curled her fingers around those hard, wet shoulders?

Where was it as his kiss deepened and Mina not only opened for him but slicked her tongue against his, curling, inviting, *demanding* more?

She'd learned a lot from their earlier kiss. It had blasted away the little she'd thought she knew about kissing. Her limited experience hadn't prepared her for Alexei's wholesale takeover of her senses.

He didn't even touch her, except for his lips and tongue, but that was enough to create a sensual storm. Mina was swept away, clinging to his shoulders for support and to prevent him pulling back.

She'd been the one to withdraw last time. His hand on her breast had broken the moment, terrifying her. Not because he'd overstepped the bounds. But because Mina had been overwhelmed by how much she'd wanted more. How reckless he made her.

Stupid. Thoughtless.

The words lost their sting as Alexei's heat swamped her and she felt his body all down hers. He angled his head for better access to her mouth and growled his appreciation as she sucked his tongue hard.

Had she ever heard such a sexy sound? It made her nipples pebble and heat blossom at the apex of her thighs where she felt an achy emptiness.

Mina might have an impulsive streak but in some things she was innately cautious. She'd never given herself to a man. Never been attracted enough to trust someone so intimately. Never been so swept away that it wasn't a matter of *if* but *when* she surrendered.

Alexei made her feel more than she'd thought possible. *That* scared her. He didn't.

Fingers still curled into his shoulder muscles,

she turned her head, breaking the kiss. The sound of their ragged breathing filled the air.

'You don't really want me here.' Mina struggled to find an argument that would end this.

'But I need you here.' His words were hot on her sensitised skin, his mouth moving against her cheek in a caress that made her tremble.

'Only as bait to lure him.' She gasped the words, trying to catch her breath. Trying to find the strength to push Alexei away. If she had any self-respect, she'd stop this.

His fingers gripped her chin, inexorably turning her head. Alexei was so close she fell into that malachite gaze.

'He can go to hell. All I can think about is you.' Alexei frowned, his look almost savage, his breathing as uneven as Mina's. 'If you'd been seriously hurt out there...' He shook his head. 'You have no idea how I felt, thinking about that.'

Mina read the echo of her own stark emotions in Alexei's flared nostrils, tight jaw, grim line of mouth and shadowed eyes.

'Believe me, I know.' Mina couldn't hold back the words. 'When I thought about how I'd put you at risk I felt sick.' Alexei's hand softened against her face, palming her cheek, inviting her to turn her head into his touch. She did, luxuriating in the comfort of it, even as it sent a buzz of adrenalin ricocheting through her body. 'It's crazy. I don't even know you—'

'And you don't like me,' he added with a wry tilt of his mouth.

'I don't think this is about liking.' What she felt came from a deep, vital part of herself and it demanded honesty. She was beyond prevarication.

The hint of humour in his expression died. 'Carissa, I—'

'No!' She pressed her fingers to his mouth, desperate to stop his words. Mina couldn't bear for him to call her by her friend's name. Not when she trembled on the brink of something so huge. 'Don't say anything. No more words, please.'

There were lies enough between them. But what she felt, however unexpected, was real. More real than anything she'd felt for any other man.

It had to be just sex. It couldn't be anything more. Yet this felt as unstoppable as sunrise. As wondrous as a child's smile.

She could no more turn her back on this than she could stop the storm outside.

Even if she could, she didn't want to.

It was time.

Instead of smiling, Alexei's expression grew

more serious. There was no triumph in his eyes, or greedy anticipation, just a steady regard that told her he felt the same.

Or was she impossibly naive, painting her own wash on circumstances?

Before she could decide, Alexei bent, slid an arm around her back and another behind her legs, and lifted her off the floor. Mina slipped her hands around his neck, torn between dismay at being hoisted high against his hard chest and quivering delight at how strong and sure he felt. How utterly feminine he made her feel.

She'd never ceded control to any man. Had resisted it, she now realised, after seeing so many acquaintances pushed into unwanted, arranged marriages. Her sister included. Now she discovered the delight of being with a man whose physical strength far surpassed hers. Surprisingly she didn't feel vulnerable but treasured.

He carried her out of the bathroom and Mina's pulse quickened as they approached her bed. But Alexei kept going, through the door and down the corridor that formed the spine of the house. Towards the master suite.

The hall was gloomy and the wind sounded like the malevolent howl of the desert djinns her nurse had told her about when she was little. Mina shivered.

'We're safe here.' Alexei must have sensed her thoughts. 'The main house is built to withstand worse than this.' He stopped walking and fixed her with that steady gaze. 'But if you prefer, we could sit this out in the basement storm shelter.'

He was giving her the opportunity to change her mind. One last chance at sanity.

For answer Mina slid her fingers into his wet hair and tugged his head down, pressing her lips to his. She slicked her tongue along his mouth till he opened. Alexei shuddered, then gathered her closer still, his hold so tight he crushed her breathless.

When, finally, he lifted his head, she couldn't hear the wind over the thunder of her blood and Alexei had lost that veneer of calm. She read naked hunger in his dark eyes.

Mina squirmed as arousal coursed through her, coalescing in a sensation like wax melting and softening between her legs.

Then Alexei was striding down the dim hall, eating up the distance to his room.

Fleetingly Mina wondered about mentioning her inexperience, but she shied from anything that might delay or even stop what lay ahead. Besides, instinct had worked fine so far.

Alexei lowered her feet to the floor and switched on a bedside lamp. Mina had an impression of space, of furnishings the colour of parchment with azure accents, then Alexei put his hands on her waist and she had eyes for nothing but him.

His black hair glistened, wet against his skull. Lamplight highlighted the severe, beautiful angle of his cheekbones and threw into relief the stern set of his nose.

Mina's gaze dropped to his mouth, so sensual and generous. Her heart dipped and she felt again the liquid rush of desire.

She swayed closer, grabbing his shirt. Of their own volition her fingers began undoing his buttons. Gone was the deft quickness of a woman who worked with her hands. She fumbled first one, then another, but Alexei didn't help, just stood, still as a breathing statue.

A breathing, hot statue of majestic proportions. Mina finally slid the final button free and pushed her hands between the open edges of his shirt. Damp heat, heavily moulded muscle, the crispness of chest hair, the quick throb of his powerful heartbeat.

A quiver ran through him as she slid her palms over his pectorals to his collarbone, pushing the shirt wide across his shoulders and down his arms. Alexei shrugged and it fell, leaving Mina in possession of a view that stole her breath.

She wanted to sculpt him. She wanted to run her hands over every contour and angle, from the heavy weight of muscle to the masculine symmetry of ribs and hips. She wanted to taste him, to see if he responded to her lips on his body.

'My turn.' Alexei caught her as she leaned closer. She was still processing his words when he tugged her T-shirt up. Obediently Mina lifted her arms and tossed it free.

His gaze dipped to her breasts. Mina felt her nipples harden and, realising her bra was probably transparent when wet, felt heat rise in her throat. Not from embarrassment, but from a cocktail of pride and daring at Alexei's expression. There was glazed heat in his eyes, while his tight mouth and flared nostrils spoke of immense control.

'Not pink?' His voice was hoarse, as if his throat had dried.

To her surprise Mina found herself pushing her shoulders back, inviting him to stare. Was this the same woman who never flaunted herself?

Who found male attention more often a nuisance than anything else?

But this was different. With Alexei nothing was as it had been.

'No, not pink.' Her bra and matching knickers were of silk and cobweb lace in dark anthracite grey. The combination of bold colour and soft, exquisitely worked fabric was pure Mina, who'd never chosen a pastel in her life.

'I like it.' His mouth barely moved on the words. 'Take it off.' His voice was as harsh as the sanding block she used to finish a stone sculpture.

Suddenly his eyes were on hers, the cool green no longer cool. Mina felt a judder pass through her, something shared between them. Understanding. Desire. Desperation.

Not allowing time for second thoughts, Mina reached back and unclipped her bra. Her breasts swung free as she tugged it off. A flash of exaltation filled her as she watched Alexei's expression, his sudden swallow, the tension in his jaw.

Alexei might be more experienced, he might be bigger and stronger, but Mina had her own power.

Then a hard palm centred over her nipple, closing gently on her breast, squeezing with just the right amount of pressure, and Mina's self-satisfaction disintegrated.

Something zipped like lightning from her breast to her womb, leaving a scorched trail. Her knees rocked and for a second she wondered if they'd hold her, till Alexei curled his arm around her waist and pulled her close. Her hips pressed the damp denim of his jeans.

Her breath was a choked moan and his mouth rucked up in a smile that looked as if it bordered on pain.

Still, he worked her breast and Mina felt something vital inside her give and break free. She leaned closer, desperate for more, overwhelmed at the escalating pace of desire.

Alexei pressed his mouth to the side of her neck, near the curve that opened to her shoulder. But instead of kissing, he grazed with his teeth, then nipped gently. Mina jumped as another electric charge passed through her, exacerbating the neediness low in her body. She wriggled against him, desperate for relief.

Her hands went to his jeans, flicking the button undone as if she'd done this so many times before. Then his zip, harder to open because of the erection straining the fabric. Finally she succeeded, inserting her hands between his hips and the fabric, drawing slowly down.

A shudder passed through him, his hold tightening, then the hot length of him sprang free to rest against her.

Mina moulded him with her hands, her touch inquisitive, wondering, testing the fascinating weight and surprising silk-over-steel sensation.

But not for long. Alexei captured her wrists, pulling them away. He muttered something under his breath and stepped back. But before she could protest he shucked his shoes and shoved his jeans down.

Mina had thought his upper body beautiful, his erection arresting. But those thighs, even the carved shape of his knees and, when he turned away from her, the bunch of muscled buttocks... She breathed deep and felt herself quiver and quicken. An artist's response to beauty melded with a woman's need. It was an irresistible combination.

When he turned back from the bedside table, he was rolling on a condom. It was the most erotic thing Mina had ever seen.

She wanted, how she wanted.

But suddenly she couldn't bring herself to move or touch. Her feet were welded to the floor and a curious weakness stole through her. Nerves? Now?

Alexei didn't smile as he flicked open the snap at the top of her shorts. His expression was serious as he tugged the zip down. Mina shifted but not from embarrassment or doubt. She found herself tilting her pelvis towards him, till he cupped her with that big hand and she felt pressure just where she needed it.

So good. She closed her eyes as they rolled back, which meant she didn't see him push the last of her clothes down her legs. When she opened them again he was crouched before her, undoing the tiny buckles on those flimsy pink sandals.

Mina's legs were so wobbly she put her hands on Alexei's shoulders as he slipped off her shoes, then freed her shorts and underwear.

She stood naked before him, primed and ready. Mina felt the moisture between her legs, knew it would help when they came together, yet still Alexei didn't rise. Instead he surprised her by leaning in, dipping his head to the soft curls above her thighs.

Obeying the silent pressure of his hands, Mina moved one leg wider. She heard a grunt of approval, then nothing but a roaring in her ears as he touched his tongue to her. More than touched. Dipped and swirled and probed.

Mina's fingers turned to talons, raking his shoulders. Her knees shook so much she'd have fallen if not for his grip. And then, suddenly, coaxed with a delicacy and precision that spoke of generous expertise, Mina exploded into rapture. Lights blurred behind closed lids, piercing pleasure filled her, so sweet it made her ache and throb, so shocking she felt as if the world collapsed in on itself.

Or maybe that was her. She was no longer standing, but lying on the bed and the soaring, intense orgasm kept going as Alexei pressed his hand where his mouth had been and kissed his way up her stomach and ribs to her breast.

Mina sucked in a desperate gasp. She'd died and gone to paradise. But surely she couldn't take any more delight.

Which proved how innocent she truly was. For Alexei proceeded to illustrate with ease exactly how much more she could enjoy.

Her senses blurred. The only constant was the heat of Alexei naked against her, the tender touch of those hard hands, his scent, sharp and addictive, and the taste of salty skin as she kissed his shoulder, chest, throat, wherever she could reach.

Finally, when she thought she'd go mad with desperation, he gave in to the urging of her hands and restless body and settled between her legs. Mina lifted her knees, wrapping her calves around his waist and linking her ankles. She was so ready, she wouldn't allow any more delay.

Alexei's hot eyes held hers as he tested her then, with one hard thrust, embedded himself deep within.

Mina's breath snared in her throat and for a shocking moment she couldn't get enough oxygen. She read Alexei's puzzlement in that furrowed brow and questioning eyes. But her attention was on her tight lungs and even tighter body. She felt pinned to the bed, fuller than she'd imagined possible. She couldn't move, couldn't possibly—

'Breathe. Slowly, sweetheart.' Alexei's voice infiltrated her stunned brain. His fingers trailed her cheek in a touch that was as delicate as a butterfly wing, so different from the invasive weight of his possession.

Belatedly Mina sucked in air. Relieved, she breathed in and out with him, watching his mouth, watching the flare of his nostrils and matching her efforts to his. Gradually her frantic pulse eased a fraction, the fog in her brain clearing.

Panic subsided and she felt her taut muscles soften. There was no pain. Simply surprise, a sensation that was neither good nor bad.

Alexei moved, beginning to pull back, and despite her reaction a moment before, Mina couldn't bear the thought of him leaving her. This might feel strange but she craved more. She tightened her legs around him, digging her fingers into his shoulders.

'Don't go.'

He shook his head, his wavy black hair flopping endearingly over his brow, making him appear younger, despite the lines of tension etching his features. 'Don't worry, sweetheart. I'm not going far.' Holding her gaze, he withdrew, then, at the last moment thrust forward.

'Oh.' Mina blinked, stunned at the fizz of appreciation his movement stirred.

His smile looked close to a grimace. 'Exactly.' He repeated the movement, this time with a little more force, and the fizz became of zap of arousal.

With each tilt of his hips, each surge towards her, Alexei kept his attention on her, reading her reaction in her expression. As she'd guessed, her body knew what to do, even if she didn't. Already she'd learned to tilt her pelvis to accommodate him. Yet Mina wanted to do more. She wanted to be as generous as he'd been. She wanted to see him lost to the world, floating in rapture.

'What can I do to make it better for you?'

His laugh was a harsh, grating sound. 'Nothing. It's already too good.'

Mina frowned, fighting the urge to acquiesce and simply enjoy the wonderful new sensations. Her knowledge was all theoretical but it gave her a few ideas.

The next time Alexei thrust, she didn't just grip him with her thighs, but clenched her inner muscles too. She was rewarded with a hoarse gasp that bordered on a groan. Beads of sweat broke out on his brow and he shuddered.

Delighted, Mina tugged at his right hand, lifting it from the bed and clamping it over her breast. It stayed there, moulding and plucking and adding to her pleasure.

Another thrust, another squeeze and this time Mina had to swallow a gasp of delight. Her tactic worked, she could see it in Alexei's febrile, almost vacant stare and the way his fluid movements grew suddenly jerky.

Then he seemed to gather himself. His eyes focused on hers and his mouth opened. 'Car—'

No! Not another woman's name now.

In a flash she reached up and drew his head down, kissing him with all the desperate yearning he'd awakened. Mina sucked his tongue deep into her mouth, palming the back of his head, drawing him closer with her whole body.

Suddenly Alexei's control broke. Hard fingers dug into her buttock as he angled her body higher. He took over the kiss, driving into her mouth as he drove into her body, with a shocking, wonderful synchronicity that pushed her straight over the edge into spasms of ecstasy.

His body was steely hard, his movements convulsive, and the moan of release she swallowed sounded as if it had been drawn from the depths of his soul. Through it all they stayed locked together as one. Each explosion of sensation in one echoed in the other.

Finally, when the last shudders subsided to tiny tremors, Alexei broke their kiss and rolled onto his side, pulling her with him.

Struggling, Mina opened weighted eyelids. That sea of green engulfed her again and this time she didn't mind. She felt weightless and languorous and so very, very good.

No, it was more than that. It felt as if they were one. It was remarkable, far more fantastic than she'd believed possible. Surely there was some magic involved that made this more than a mere physical act. It felt...momentous.

Slowly she smiled, though even that took too much energy. 'You were right. There's definitely chemistry.'

CHAPTER TEN

ALEXEI STARED INTO those beautiful, sleepy, sherry-brown eyes and didn't know whether to laugh or run for the hills.

Except running wasn't an option. Problems had to be confronted. And no matter how delightful she was in his bed, Carissa Carter was a problem with a capital *P*.

He should be annoyed she hadn't warned him she was a virgin. He should be worried that in her inexperience she could misread great sex for something more. He should be checking the storm shutters and weather warnings. And he definitely should be disposing of the condom.

Alexei stayed exactly where he was, surrounded by firm, silky heat. Her legs around his waist were a perfect fit. His eyes flickered shut as he replayed the moment when she'd gripped him hard, everywhere, and he'd been ready to explode like an untested kid.

Speaking of untested... He opened his eyes and

focused on the dreamy smile still lingering on Carissa's lush, reddened mouth. He recalled the taste of her, the hungry, avid kiss that had sent him hurtling over the edge. It made him throb within her and he saw her eyes pop wide.

It surprised him too, the fact that there was a spark of life when he'd spilled himself so completely.

'Are you okay? Are you sore?'

Move. You need to leave her alone.

Yet he couldn't bring himself to do it yet. Not when she was so inviting, clinging as if she never wanted to let him go.

Alexei had never liked post-coital pillow talk. He kept a definite line between sex and friendship, not giving lovers the idea they might be in his life long-term. And still he couldn't bring himself to move.

She shook her head, her dark hair, still damp, sliding around her shoulders and onto the pillow. She wore not a trace of make-up and her only adornment was the pair of tiny, intricate gold earrings she'd worn since she arrived.

Yet she was one of the most alluring women he'd seen. Not a perfect beauty, but then the supposedly perfect beauties he'd known weren't either. The more time Alexei spent with Carissa, the more fascinated he was by the line of her cheekbones, her lush mouth and speaking eyes.

'No, I'm not sore.' She clenched her muscles, gripping him tight, and Alexei felt himself quicken. That should be impossible.

But he was learning to expect the unexpected with Carissa.

'Still, you should have told me I was your first.' The words filled him with a mix of feelings. Privilege. Triumph. And, he was stunned to discover, possessiveness. As if he wanted to lay claim to her.

Carissa shrugged, the movement dragging her breasts teasingly across his torso. Another shimmer of tension arrowed to his groin.

'Maybe. But I was afraid you might stop.'

Did she have any idea what her words did to him? How they encouraged the half-formed lascivious, proprietorial thoughts in his befuddled brain?

'It would have taken much more than that to stop me.' He tried to imagine pulling back and couldn't. As well he hadn't been put to the test. Alexei prided himself on mastery over his animal instincts. But with Carissa that untamed side came to the fore. He was tempted to see how far this gathering arousal could take him, take them.

Witnessing Carissa lose herself so totally, spread before him like a delectable feast, had been better than anything he remembered for a long time.

Too long. He told himself it had been all work and no play recently. That was why the sex had seemed so preternaturally spectacular.

'But you enjoyed it.' It was couched as a statement but Alexei read the question in her eyes. It was a timely reminder that this was new to her. She had no reference point, no way of knowing that they'd shared something out of the ordinary.

How had that happened? Why had such a sensual woman remained celibate? Alexei had no doubt her responses were genuine, not feigned. She enjoyed sex as much as he did. Her patent enthusiasm had added spice to his pleasure.

Why end her virginity now, with him? Because, like him, she'd been unable to resist the elemental attraction that had sparked since she stepped over his threshold?

No, even before that. Alexei had felt it as she stood, arms akimbo, surveying his house. When she'd stared up at him with such arrogant confidence. He'd never experienced anything like it—so instantaneous and compulsive.

But the question remained, why end her virginity today?

Because it could be a useful negotiating tool? The thought eddied like a circling shark.

Did she think to convince him to go easy on her father, despite his crime? His mouth tightened. Distrust was hard to shake when it was so ingrained.

'Oh, yes. I definitely enjoyed the sex, Carissa.'

Something passed across her features. Something he couldn't define, but it made heat score her cheeks. Instantly he wished he'd chosen his words more carefully. No matter what her ultimate motivation, she'd been generous with him and deserved the same. He prided himself on being a considerate lover. But even to him, the words had sounded harsh, almost dismissive.

With a stab of self-loathing he stroked her hair back from her face. 'Thank you, Carissa. It was wonderful. *You* were wonderful.'

It was true. What they'd shared was beyond anything he recalled. Was he so jaded it had taken sex with a virgin to turn him on?

No, the truth lay elsewhere. It was something about Carissa and the way she made him feel. She was different. Enticing and provoking and more besides. Alexei breathed deep, drawing in her evocative spice-and-cinnamon scent. He could easily become addicted to it. To her.

Lightly he grazed the base of her neck with his teeth. Carissa shivered and clutched at him.

Alexei closed his eyes, savouring her responsiveness and the prospect of more voluptuous pleasure. It would be a simple thing to coax her into more. As he thought it, he recognised the tightening in his groin. He could stay here and sate himself. She was willing. He felt it in the way she arched into him, and in her quickened heartbeat that throbbed against his chest.

Yet he couldn't do it.

He was the experienced one. He was the one who'd initiated this. It was up to him to act responsibly. To be considerate.

Dispose of the condom. Let her rest. All sensible, but it was difficult to make his body obey his brain.

With one last open-mouthed kiss on her satiny flesh, Alexei sighed and pulled back. He gritted his teeth, for in his semi-aroused state the friction was a powerful inducement to stay where he was. As were Carissa's limbs around his body.

'Must you go?'

He opened his eyes to find her watching him with an expression of such disappointment he knew he'd been right. Staying here, luxuriating in her sensuality would be a mistake. It would probably leave her aching. Plus it might convince her this was more than an act of simple physical intimacy. That she should expect more than he was willing to give.

Alexei grabbed her wrists from behind his neck and drew them down between their bodies. Her soft breasts and plum-coloured nipples brushed his hands, diverting him as erotic energy zapped through him.

He was crazy, denying himself. It was clear from her hitched breath and dilated eyes that Carissa wanted more.

But his conscience wouldn't let him stay. She'd change her mind if he made her chafed and sore.

'Be honest with me. Did I hurt you?'

She shook her head. 'No. It felt…odd but not painful.'

'Odd?' His brows drew together and she laughed, a rich chuckle that reminded him of melted chocolate and sunshine.

'Unusual. But good. Very, very good.' Her smile was two parts sultry seductress and one part carefree woman.

Alexei was intrigued by the latter. It struck him that he wanted to learn about that woman, discover what made her tick. He couldn't meld her in his mind with a conniving accomplice to theft he'd imagined.

'Good. That gives us something to aim for next time.'

Her smile lit her face. 'There'll be a next time?'

'Oh, yes.' Alexei wasn't strong enough to abstain permanently.

He lifted one of her hands and kissed it, starting on the back of her hand and working his way around her wrist, where her pulse fluttered wildly, to her palm. He licked it slowly, savouring, and watched her shiver.

'I want it to be soon,' she whispered. Her eyes were sultry and enticing. Alexei had to force himself to move away.

'As soon as you've rested.'

'I'm not tired!'

Was that a pout? Heaven help him—that mouth tempted him to forget good intentions.

'Perhaps *I* am.' It was a fabrication but better than telling her he acted for her own good. She hated any hint he had power over her. Except when he'd had her beneath him.

Her gaze shifted down his body and his erection stirred. 'You don't *look* tired.'

Alexei muffled a bark of laughter. She was right. He felt energised.

He should simply get up and leave her to rest, but that was beyond his powers. What he needed was a distraction. 'How's your hand?' He angled it to inspect the bandage.

'I can't feel any pain.'

Alexei darted a glance at her. It would probably hurt later when the endorphins faded. It was a nasty gash. But then, he'd realised as he treated her, she'd had a few accidents in the past.

He slid his thumb over the fine skin at the back of her hand, seeing two tiny scars, faded now. And on the palm some rougher patches, as if it had seen work instead of simply lotions and manicures.

Alexei turned her hand over again, considering the supple strength in those slim fingers, the lack of jewellery, the short nails.

Why hadn't he noticed? This wasn't the hand of a pampered socialite.

'What sort of art do you do?'

It was only because he held her that he noticed her flinch. It was momentary, so brief he almost thought he was mistaken. But now her hand was stiff, not relaxed. His curiosity deepened.

'All sorts of things. Drawing, oils, sculpting, even some pottery.'

His sixth sense stirred. She was being evasive. Why?

'Surely you specialise in one? Don't successful artists focus their energies?'

Mina read the acuteness in Alexei's gaze and wondered at his instinct for pinpointing vulnerability. It was as if he knew exactly what to ask to uncover the truth. Carissa was a successful graphic artist but Mina's expertise and passion lay in sculpture.

No wonder he was such a successful businessman with that uncannily accurate instinct. Or was it a fluke? Was she overreacting?

In the distance she heard the furious rush of the storm. It echoed the abrupt warning clamour surging within her.

Mina told herself it was just as well she was no longer crammed up so close against him he might feel her response to his words. Even so she was still desperate for his caresses, for more of the glory they'd shared. That had challenged her preconceptions about him and made her wonder if Alexei was someone more than simply a demanding tycoon, used to getting his way.

Or was that her bias? The virgin fixating on the man who'd introduced her to sex? Because what she'd experienced with Alexei had felt almost transcendental, as if they'd achieved a union that was unique and precious.

Her thoughts were in turmoil, her emotions all over the place. She was in danger of letting feelings cloud her judgement. But, oh, how she wanted to bask in what Alexei made her feel!

'Carissa?'

'Sorry. Yes, artists do tend to specialise.'

What harm was there, telling him about her work? Remarkably, this was the man who hadn't bothered to look at Carissa's photo before bringing her here. If he wasn't interested enough to do that, he wouldn't have checked out her work.

It was a startling reminder that, despite the intimacy of the moment, they were still opponents in a dangerous game. That left a sour tang on Mina's tongue and an ache in her middle.

It grew harder and harder to reconcile that imperious tycoon with the man lying naked beside her.

'And your specialty?'

Mina hesitated, then took the plunge. She was finding some success but it wasn't as if her work was well known. Soon, hopefully. 'I sculpt.'

'*Now* it makes sense.' His rueful smile made her heart hammer and warmth unfurl inside. It was as if they shared a private joke. Mina realised she wanted more of this. More of Alexei's warmth and understanding.

'Saving the sail sculpture? It's a masterpiece. I couldn't leave it.'

He nodded. 'Of course not. I see that now.' His tone held no rancour, just understanding. Why not? It was obvious the man loved sculpture too. The pieces scattered through his home were superb.

'I was working in Paris on ideas for something similar, but with stylised birds' wings that will move, propelled by the wind. It's far more difficult than you'd imagine.' If she could bring it off it would be perfect for Jeirut's first royal art exhibition. Mina had promised Ghizlan she'd contribute something special and she could imagine the piece at the Palace of the Winds.

'I'd like to see that.'

'I've got drawings...' Mina closed her mouth over her eager response as doubt welled. What else was in her current sketchbook? Anything that would give away her true identity?

'I'd be fascinated to see them.'

Slowly Mina nodded. She'd like to show him

and hear his thoughts. She suspected his response would be informed but honest.

'I'll check to see if I have them with me,' she said finally. Mina looked away, hating the dishonesty of her situation. She had the strongest desire to strip away the lies. To know him properly and have him know her.

She wanted...more.

Except Carissa relied on her.

Mina swallowed, bitterness filling her mouth.

'Are you sure you're okay, Carissa?'

She suppressed a shiver. Even being called by her friend's name felt wrong.

'Of course.' Mina darted a glance towards him, but didn't quite meet his eyes. 'Maybe you're right. I think I need a rest after all.'

It was another lie. For Mina felt sparking with life and eager for more of Alexei's loving. What did that say about her? She'd known the man mere days!

She knew so little about him. Except that he felt deeply. That he abhorred cheats, was impatient yet surprisingly kind, determined, outrageous and used to getting his own way. That when he made love to her she felt as if she could fly and that everything in the world was bright and fresh. When she was with Alexei everything was more intense.

With him she had the strangest feeling she could be more herself than she could with anyone else. And that wasn't just about sex. The realisation was disquieting.

'I'll leave you to rest.' He rose and Mina had to clench her hands rather than reach out and draw him back.

She missed the warmth of Alexei's powerful body and the feeling of oneness. She wanted to see that smile in his eyes and bask in that wonderment again.

'Okay?' His hand brushed her cheek and delight coursed through her. Such a simple gesture, yet it affected her profoundly.

When had she let anyone close? Mina had spent so long hoarding her emotions to herself, first as self-protection, then because she'd focused on achieving her dream. Only Carissa had suspected Mina's air of assurance and practicality masked innate loneliness.

Mina looked up into Alexei's alert green gaze and her chest pinched tight.

'Yes, I'm okay.' And she was. Despite the circumstances, despite the lies between them that she so wanted to obliterate. In this, she reminded herself, she had no choice...yet. But soon she'd be free to explain. 'Just tired.' And suddenly that too was true. Mina stifled a cracking yawn.

'Sleep then, lover. I'll be back later.'

Mina settled her head on the pillow and watched him go, hearing that *lover* as an echo that refused to die.

Tall, shoulders back, he sauntered towards the bathroom with the grace of an athlete utterly at home in his skin. What exercise did he do to keep so fit?

Her gaze traced the curving sweep of his spine, the tight bunch of his backside, the powerful, well-formed legs.

Mina wanted to sculpt him. Almost as much as she wanted to run her hands over all that warm, muscled flesh.

Her last thought before sleep took her was that she enjoyed being with Alexei Katsaros. Too much.

Alexei checked the house, the generator and the radio. The storm had hit quickly but was even now easing. The forecast predicted it would pass over soon.

Yet all the time he busied himself with what had to be done, his thoughts tracked back to Carissa. How she'd felt in his arms, in his bed, her body yielding and soft yet strong. Her slick heat driving him out of his mind. And those little growls of pleasure she gave. The memory sent a judder of longing through him.

Which was why he spent as much time as he could away from the bedroom. He knew next to nothing about virgins. There hadn't been many in the rough streets where he'd grown up. But common sense dictated he should let her sleep.

Yet an hour later he was back in his room, staring down at the woman who'd turned his life upside down in a mere couple of days. Unbelievable that it was such a short time. It felt as if she'd been in his world much longer.

He drew a steadying breath and shoved his hands in his pockets as he surveyed her, sprawled across his bed. In the lamplight her glossy, dark hair splayed around her shoulders and her lithe, gold-toned body was a masterpiece, more alluring than any work of art.

Alexei was surprised at the depth of his desire to possess her. Not just possess her body, as he fully intended to when she woke, but to claim this woman as... What? His mistress? Carter's daughter shouldn't be for him.

Yet, when he was with her, it wasn't her father's wrongdoing that came to mind. It was the tug of something else that drew him inexorably. Desire. Attraction. Curiosity. Appreciation that she gave as good as she got. And for her humour, her unpretentious attitude, the way she'd developed a bond of friendship with Marie and Henri so quickly.

So much about her intrigued.

She mumbled and rolled over. Alexei's thoughts frayed as he watched those tip-tilted breasts jiggle. The curve from breasts to narrow waist, then out to her hip was so sweet it stole his breath. One slim leg slid over the other, almost hiding that V of dark hair. The memory of their coupling, of her virginal tightness and shocked ecstasy, created a jolt of triumph so strong it flattened his good intentions. She'd been delectable, so charmingly enthusiastic.

Alexei's resolve disintegrated as a wave of need slammed into him. He'd done his best, he told himself as he reefed his shirt up. He really had, he assured himself as he reached for the box of condoms in the bedside table.

But he was a man, not a saint.

Minutes later he gathered her to him, his chest against her back, his legs curved into hers from behind, the burning heat of his groin hard against the sweet curve of her rump.

'Alexei?' She turned her head, her hair falling back against his chest, a sliding silk curtain that tickled and aroused.

'Yes?' He slid his hand around to cup her breast. Immediately her nipple puckered, hard against his palm. The tension in his lower body screwed another notch tighter.

'I'm glad you're here.' She sounded breathless.

'So am I.' He bumped his groin against her and felt her chuckle resonate through him. Her hand covered his, pressing down as she arched into his touch.

'Are we going to have sex again now?'

Her words sent a flurry of need rushing through him. 'If you're not sore.' If she was he'd have to be inventive. He was definitely up to that challenge.

'I'm not.' She turned, trying to roll towards him but Alexei held her where she was. 'Don't you want to be on top?'

The question reminded him how inexperienced she was. That he was the first man she'd been with. This time the surge of erotic excitement was so profound it threatened to blow the back off his skull. Or make him come before he was ready. Her soft, warm flesh against him was almost too good.

'There are other ways,' he murmured and bit her neck. She sighed and angled her head to give him better access. Alexei released her breast and arrowed his hand down past her ribs, her belly, to her hidden core. He found her slick and hot, unmistakeably ready. His erection throbbed needily and Carissa pushed back against him.

'Show me,' she demanded, fingers stroking along his arm, then back up, sending shivers across his flesh to coalesce at his nape and groin. He liked her bold acceptance of pleasure.

Alexei inserted one knee between hers, opening her legs a little. He nudged between her thighs, positioning himself.

'You don't have to do anything but, if you like, in a minute you can push back when I...'

His words died as he thrust forward, slowly at first. But then she wriggled, taking him deeper with a sexy little shimmy of her hips and Alexei found himself bucking hard and strong, as deep as he could go.

Behind his closed lids stars burst. So good. It felt so unbelievably good that it took a second to realise Carissa had gone rigid in his arms.

Was he too much? Had he hurt her? Heart

pounding, Alexei began to withdraw, silently cursing. He should have taken more time, pleasured her more.

Her hand clamped the back of his upper thigh like a talon.

'Don't!'

'Carissa?' He frowned, disorientated by the contradiction of her sharp voice and the clench of her inner muscles that threatened to destroy the last vestiges of thought.

For answer she drove back against him, impaling herself. 'That feels…'

'What?' For the life of him he couldn't move away. His hand circled her hip, then crept up to her breast. Her breath caught. 'How does it feel?'

'Wonderful,' she whispered. 'So wonderful.'

And that, to Alexei's amazement, was all it took for him to feel the fierce rush of power as a climax tore through him. He barely had time to ease back and surge again, right to the heart of her, and hear her laugh of shocked pleasure. Then the madness was upon him, fire in his blood, a roaring shout of ecstasy and the hard pump of him spilling into her beautiful body.

It took a long time to come down from the high. Aftershocks rocked him, setting off Carissa's orgasm, which in turned drove him on a desperate, slowly diminishing cycle of delight.

Finally, what seemed a lifetime later, he slumped against her, head in the curve of her neck, arms encircling her as if to prevent her leaving. Dazed, Alexei realised he didn't have enough energy even to pull away and lie on his back. His body was locked with hers and there it would stay.

'I think…' Her words were so faint they were a shadow of sound.

'Yes?' Alexei struggled to focus.

'I think I could get addicted to this.'

His mouth curved against the satiny skin of her neck. He knew the feeling. Sex with Carissa Carter was either the best idea he'd ever had or the worst mistake of his life.

CHAPTER ELEVEN

MINA STRETCHED, BLINKING, and surfaced from one of the deepest sleeps of her life. She felt wonderful, apart from a little tenderness. When she recalled why she was tender, she smiled. So this was what all the fuss was about!

Being with Alexei was unlike anything she'd imagined.

Better. Wonderful. She felt...different.

She rolled over to find the storm shutters open. Beyond the windows was the vivid blaze of green foliage, scarlet flowers and turquoise water. A songbird trilled and the hush of waves on sand proved yesterday's maelstrom was over.

How long had she slept? Long enough for Alexei to be up and about.

Cravenly she wished he hadn't gone. If she'd woken wrapped around him, she wouldn't have a chance to think. She'd be too busy exploring *him*. Carnal excitement filled her.

In his absence thoughts crammed her head,

vying for supremacy over her feeling of contentment.

With a sigh she stuffed pillows behind her and sat up. The fine linen sheets felt heavy over her sensitised skin, grazing her nipples as she tucked the fabric under her arms. Making her remember last night in delicious detail.

If Alexei walked in now, she'd fling the sheet aside and indulge in her new favourite pastime. Sex.

Except, what they'd shared seemed much more than a mere physical coupling. It had felt...

Mina shook her head, her hair sliding around her shoulders. Whatever it had felt like, it had to stop.

She caught her lip between her teeth. It would be easy to tell herself she wasn't thinking straight after such mind-boggling pleasure but she couldn't escape her conscience. Responsibility, doing right, had been drummed into her from childhood.

Despite what her eager body urged, it wasn't right to sleep with Alexei while he believed her to be someone else!

A selfish part of her wanted to thrust that aside. After all, he'd given Carissa no choice. He deserved whatever he got for his high-handed actions. And yet... Even in so short a time, she knew he was far more complex than the bogey-man they'd made him into. For one thing, Carissa's father had stolen from him, on a large scale. Who wouldn't be irate in the circumstances? Alexei was a victim of crime and deserved sympathy, not more treachery.

Besides, this wasn't a question of Alexei's culpability but hers. This masquerade didn't sit well with Mina's conscience. True, she did it for the best reasons, but it was still a lie. It was one thing to be swept off her feet in heightened passion and not reveal the truth. It was another to share Alexei's bed while duping him. She'd feel cheap and tainted, prolonging that lie while they were physically intimate.

Mina hugged herself as a chill enveloped her. She wanted to be selfish and have more of what she'd had last night.

But she couldn't, not without telling Alexei who she was.

Her conscience urged her to find Alexei and reveal the truth. Surely he'd understand. He wouldn't insist on dragging Carissa into this.

Then she remembered his fury when he'd spoken of Carissa's father. That adamantine set of Alexei's jaw as he'd spoken of retribution. A chill spread through her like mountain frost. Mina hoped he'd change his mind but she couldn't guarantee it. There was a chance he'd go through with his plans for Carissa.

Nausea swirled in her stomach and bile rose in her throat at the idea of Alexei with Carissa. *Marrying* her.

She wanted to scream that it wasn't possible. He wouldn't do that, not now, he'd more or less admitted that had been a ploy to get her here. But there were no guarantees. Alexei was a powerful man used to getting what he wanted.

She couldn't risk it. Carissa had pleaded for another couple of days. If Mina revealed the truth now Alexei might still use her friend as a pawn. Mina hated to think it but she had to face facts.

Which left her lusting for a man she couldn't fully trust. Lying to a man she liked more than she'd expected. Yearning for—

Mina thrust aside the sheet and scrambled out of bed. Two things were clear. She couldn't tell Alexei who she was until she knew Carissa was safe with Pierre. And in the meantime, honour demanded Mina didn't sleep with Alexei again.

'Alexei?'

He looked up from the tray he was filling and

saw her framed in the kitchen doorway. His heart did a crazy somersault.

She wore a miniskirt the colour of ripe watermelon and a sleeveless white shirt that tied at the waist, emphasising her slenderness. There was plenty of honey-toned skin on display but it was her hair, a dark cloud around her shoulders, and her glowing eyes, that captivated.

Heat scudded through him. Desire. Satisfaction.

He'd had her all night but that hadn't sated his need.

She was delectable. A mix of hesitant, innocent and wanton sensualist.

'You should have stayed in bed. I was bringing brunch.' Then Alexei registered the stiff way she held herself. 'Are you okay?' He was across the room in an instant, taking her hands. 'Tell me.' Uncharacteristically, Alexei felt anxious. He told himself women lost their virginities all the time.

She swallowed and his eyes tracked the movement, senses alert. Especially when he realised she hadn't yet looked directly at him.

As he thought it, she raised her eyes, her expression serious. His gut tightened.

'I realised I never told you I'm sorry about the theft. About…my father's actions.' She grimaced.

'I didn't really think about the impact on your business. Is it a complete disaster? Will the company recover?'

Days ago Alexei would have been astounded to feel relief at her words. Yet that was what flooded him. Carissa was okay; she wasn't hurt. Or having second thoughts.

He brushed his thumbs over her wrists. 'Thank you.' Strange how something as simple as her concern, and her apology, acted as a salve on the raw wound to his pride. Because he hadn't seen the betrayal coming. Because despite excellent systems, his enterprise had still been vulnerable. 'It's…manageable.'

The theft caused major problems but not enough to destabilise the company, if handled carefully.

'Manageable?' She tilted her head, trying to read him. 'Is that code? He hasn't bankrupted you, has he?' No missing her sharp note of worry.

Alexei felt her tremble, saw her features pale. For once Carissa's thoughts were easy to read. Horror and distress.

'No, nothing like that.' He squeezed her hands. 'The company wasn't that vulnerable.'

'Good.' She nodded. 'I'm glad.'

The words were simple but he knew her well

enough to realise her sentiments were genuine. Had he really believed she'd connived with her father? Watching her now, it was hard to credit. Her concern and sincerity, clear in her eyes and taut body as well as her words, made a mockery of his doubts. She might not want to betray her father but she was innocent of his crimes.

Belatedly it hit him how difficult this had been for her.

'I've put you in a tough situation.' The words emerged without thinking. It was too late to regret his actions, especially since he couldn't regret having her here with him. But given his time over, Alexei would have taken a different approach.

Those brown eyes widened in shock. Then she lifted one shoulder. 'I've survived worse.'

She made light of it but suddenly Alexei couldn't. He felt wrong-footed. 'I acted rashly. For that I'm sorry. I assumed you knew about the theft.' When her eyes widened, he shook his head. 'My default position is not to trust anyone. I learned long ago it was safer than being disappointed.'

Even Alexei was surprised by the admission. He never explained himself. But in this case, he knew he owed her an apology.

Carissa's hands grasped his. 'Could we, maybe, put all that aside for a little?'

She looked so earnest he had to smile. Especially since, after giving an apology, Alexei wasn't quite sure where to go next. This was unfamiliar territory.

'With pleasure.' He brushed the fall of long hair off her shoulder and wrapped his other arm around her waist, tugging her close. 'I'm sure we can find something else to concentrate on.' He was leaning in to kiss her when a palm on his chest stopped him.

Carissa was staring at his collarbone, not his face. High colour flagged her cheeks.

'About that,' she said to his shirt. 'We need to take a raincheck.'

Alexei frowned. He couldn't believe it, especially as she arched sinuously against him. He could tell when a woman wanted him and Carissa did, without doubt. 'Sorry? You don't want to have sex with me?'

Her crack of laughter unlocked something tight that had formed in his chest. She shook her head. 'You're so sure of yourself.'

'With good reason.' His hand wandered lower, to the hem of her miniskirt. She stiffened.

'The fact is, I can't. I...' She lifted her face and

met his eyes with an unblinking stare. 'I've got my period.'

Disappointment seared him. It was so savage it felt like pain. Alexei opened his mouth to suggest there were ways they could, but seeing her blush deepen, recalling she'd been a virgin yesterday, he shut it again.

He dragged in a slow breath. 'I won't say I'm not disappointed. But I've survived worse.'

When she registered the echo of her own words, Carissa grinned. Suddenly she looked more like the vibrant, confident woman he knew. A weight he hadn't registered lifted from his chest. Alexei slung his arm around her shoulder and turned towards the tray he'd prepared.

'Things will seem brighter after we've eaten.'

If only food could cure sexual frustration. Because the next few days would surely test him to the limit.

'For someone who's never been on a boat you look right at home.' Alexei's voice stirred Mina from her reverie. She looked across the dinghy's bench seat to find him watching speculatively.

Three days ago his questioning stare would have made her wary, consumed with worry that he'd unmask her, for, unlike Carissa, she'd grown up in a desert kingdom with no experience of the sea. But a lot had changed. By mutual consent they didn't speak about business or revenge or the future. They existed totally in the present.

Their relationship was fragile. It could only last until the outside world intruded. But for the first time in her life it was enough just to *be*.

To be with him.

All her life, she'd strived to live up to others' expectations. First to meet her father's impossible demands. Then, finding a niche in the competitive art world, working harder than her peers to prove she hadn't achieved her initial success because of her connections.

Being with Alexei was like breathing fresh air after stale. Even though they weren't physically intimate since her lie about her period—the only way she could think of to keep him at arm's length—to her amazement he hadn't shown annoyance or frustration.

Alexei made her feel good about herself. Not because of her royal status, but because…

Because he genuinely liked her? The thought was tempting. But she couldn't afford to dwell on it. She adjusted her wide-brimmed hat.

'I'm adaptable,' she murmured, taking in the

crystalline ocean and white beach. 'Besides, the view is fantastic.'

'It sure is.' Heat simmered in his dark jade stare and Mina felt the familiar tickle of awareness. It began in the soles of her feet, climbing up her legs to swirl and intensify between her thighs, then rise, via her breasts to her throat where her breath caught.

Every time Alexei watched her she felt that same drag of muscles, the quickening, the eagerness. The sensations grew stronger with each day they spent together.

Henri and Marie hadn't returned, their boat damaged in the storm, which had hit the main island badly. They could have returned by Alexei's helicopter but it was busy on relief work and Alexei and Mina were more than able to look after themselves while the others waited for repairs.

'When you invited me out on your boat I'd pictured a massive cruiser. But this suits you better.' Her gaze drifted over his open shirt, cotton shorts and strongly muscled legs. Her pulse revved pleasantly.

Alexei shrugged, his expression wickedly knowing. 'I prefer something a little laid-back unless I have to entertain for business.'

'I can relate to that.' Mina extended one bare

leg and wriggled her toes in the sunshine. How fabulous to be free of the formal clothes appropriate to the royal court. That was something she hadn't missed in France.

'You don't like dressing up?'

'I prefer comfort.' Carissa's clothes might not be her style, but at least they included shorts and summer skirts rather than evening gowns and high heels.

Alexei reached out and stroked his finger across the arch of her foot, then up to her ankle and calf.

Mina shivered. His touch evoked a memory of his loving. It had been days now and abstinence was tough, tougher than she'd imagined.

'I can imagine you in some glamorous outfit. You'd look spectacular.'

Mina smiled. The deep timbre of his voice told her he meant every word. 'Why, thank you. I'm sure you clean up pretty well too.' He'd look stunning in formal clothes. Her insides clenched just thinking about it.

She hesitated on the brink of suggesting they go out one night in the future, he in a tuxedo, she in something slinky and feminine. Except that would mean a date and that was impossible. Once the truth came out Mina wouldn't see him again.

A sudden tightness in her chest stole her breath.

This interlude was a snatched moment out of their real lives. Neither were interested in long-term relationships. Mina had a career to build. She couldn't afford distractions. And Alexei...

'What are you thinking?'

Mina became aware of Alexei's hand, warm on her knee, of his quizzical stare fixed on her face. Regret pierced her. She wanted what they shared to last longer than a few days.

Underlying regret was surprise that Alexei understood her well enough to read her expression. Mina had spent years keeping her emotions private. She was an expert. Discovering a man who saw beyond her projected calm and sensed her disquiet should make her feel vulnerable. Yet Mina felt a thrill of excitement that Alexei was so attuned to her emotions. As if she mattered.

What did he read in her face?

Surely not her foolish longing for what could never be.

'I'm thinking you should grab that fishing line. I saw it move.'

Alexei muttered something beneath his breath and grabbed the neglected reel.

It had surprised her that he hadn't produced sleek, professional-looking fishing rods. Yet these battered hand reels, like the unpretentious boat, seemed as right for Alexei as his architect-designed home and priceless art.

He was a man who couldn't be labelled and stuck in a box. She wanted to find out more, discover what made him tick. But she resisted the temptation to pry. It could lead to places she couldn't go.

'Have you got a fish?' She leaned forward, fascinated by his sudden alertness.

'Could be.' He held the line in one sinewy hand, his attention on the water.

Mina peered over the side but couldn't see anything.

Alexei felt the tug on the line and began to reel it in.

There'd be fresh fish for dinner. Not that there was any danger of starving. Marie's well-stocked kitchen would keep them till she came back with supplies.

Strangely the thought of having company, even Marie and Henri, who were friends as much as employees, didn't appeal. He wanted more time alone with Carissa.

When she wasn't driving him to distraction with sexual frustration she was surprisingly restful company. She didn't pry or quiz him about his private life, yet Alexei had found himself talking far more than usual.

They'd discussed music and art and found more areas where their tastes overlapped than where they'd diverged. They'd discovered a shared passion for football, which made Alexei reassess his unconscious sexism. When, in the past, had he discussed sport with a lover? He'd assumed women weren't interested.

A chance comment about doing business across continents led to a discussion about the global economy and international trade. Alexei again realised he'd underestimated Carissa.

He felt ashamed that he'd been so shallow. Carissa was unique and she clearly hadn't been coached by her father. They'd veered into areas he knew were beyond Carter's expertise. Besides, Carissa had been distracted at the time, cooking. She'd got so caught up in their discussion she'd forgotten the food, till Alexei salvaged it.

She'd shrugged and admitted she wasn't much of a cook. Then she'd described her one attempt to bake a soufflé and the disastrous result. Carissa's laughter had wrapped around him like warm silk as her eyes lit at the memory.

Now she looked like an excited kid.

It hit Alexei that if she'd never been in a boat,

she'd probably never caught a fish. The thought snagged.

His childhood had been short on fun experiences after his stepfather got his feet under their table. But Alexei had one precious memory of his father teaching him to fish.

He recalled the sun on his face and the breeze off the water, and the scent of baking as his mother laid out a picnic on a blanket. Alexei remembered walking to her, one hand in his dad's big, sure grasp and the other holding up the fish he'd caught. He'd been so proud, so secure, so innocent that he'd taken everything he had for granted.

It was his final happy memory before the dark days.

'Here.' He gave Carissa the line. 'You do it.'

The excitement in her eyes hit him like a shot of liquor.

'I can feel it!' She reeled in, carefully at first, then with more confidence. 'There it is!'

Silver flashed near the water's surface but it was Carissa, animated and happy, that captured his attention. Belatedly he grabbed a scoop net and secured the fish as she brought it in.

'It's on the small side, isn't it?'

He saw her gnaw her bottom lip. Her forehead

creased as if she were unhappy. Carissa's frown deepened as the fish struggled. It seemed she had a soft heart.

'Not the biggest I've seen.' He paused, watching her. 'It's almost too small to keep.' It was a reasonable size, but Carissa was already nodding.

'Can we let it go? Give it a chance to grow? I read fish stocks are dropping because the population doesn't get a chance to reproduce.'

'*That's* why you want to let it go?'

'Well…' She shrugged. 'I liked the thrill of catching it but we're not desperate for food. I could make a salad and there's plenty of other stuff to cook.'

Alexei nodded and unhooked the fish, then put it over the side. A second later it wriggled out of his hand and away. Carissa's beaming grin as she watched was worth it.

'Thank you, Alexei.'

'No problem. Especially since you've offered to cook.' He paused and tilted his head to one side. 'I know. How about you make us a nice cheese soufflé?'

He ducked and grabbed her wrist as she swept off her sunhat and batted him with it. Then, catching her off balance, he dragged her onto his lap. The boat rocked wildly.

'That was a low blow. Just because I'm not a good cook.' She pouted but her eyes sparkled.

'But look what it got me. Who wants a fish when they can have a mermaid?'

Alexei slipped his hand behind her head and pulled out the pin securing her dark hair. He'd become adept at that. Carissa began the day by brushing her hair and securing it back from her face but Alexei preferred it loose.

His breath huffed out in satisfaction as he threaded the satiny locks through his fingers. Then he stroked lower, down her side to the couple of inches of warm, golden flesh showing between her pink shorts and cropped, polka-dotted shirt.

Carissa shivered and he saw the hard points of her nipples rise against the thin fabric. She stilled, looking up at him with a sultry, heavy-lidded look before she caught herself and tried to pull away. 'You know we can't—'

'I know. Kisses only.' Knowing she wanted him as much as he wanted her was strangely satisfying. Even though holding her and knowing he couldn't have her was an exercise in sexual frustration.

Alexei pulled her closer. He heard a splash but focused instead on that wide, delectable mouth.

'Alexei?' Carissa struggled to sit up. 'I think that was the net going over the side. Alexei?'

'Leave it.' He hauled her closer, hand splaying low on her hip. 'I've got more important things on my mind.'

Their gazes collided. A shower of sparks rained down, peppering his body with pinpricks of fire. Her expression changed and in one swift move she grabbed his shirt and tugged his face down to hers.

Alexei covered her lips with his and felt her open up. Despite the turmoil of thwarted lust, he had no desire to pull back. He couldn't recall ever feeling so…light, so unencumbered by life's burdens.

Since childhood he'd been focused on the need to survive, to succeed, to secure his place in the world. With previous lovers there'd always been a part of him that wasn't engaged. That focused on business or fending off unwanted expectations.

With Carissa, he simply enjoyed the moment. He felt just plain happy. It was a revelation.

CHAPTER TWELVE

'WHEN DID YOU know you wanted to be an artist?' Alexei watched as Carissa's sketch took shape. A couple of swift strokes and there was the outline of his hands. Another and the hint of a wrist appeared.

Watching her work, as he had these last days, left Alexei in no doubt Carissa really *was* an artist, not a spoiled daddy's girl playing at being something she wasn't.

She didn't look up. 'I never consciously decided. It's just me. I was always interested in art.'

'So your father organised for you to attend classes?'

Strange how the mention of Ralph Carter didn't make him feel that heavy twist in the gut it had before. The anger remained, and indignation, but not the seething sense of urgency. The investigator had a lead on Carter in Switzerland, but for once Alexei wasn't impatient to confront the man. That would come.

Alexei had other things to occupy him.

Carissa's brow knotted as she rubbed out a couple of lines and replaced them with others more to her liking.

'Sorry?'

'You had art lessons as a child?'

She snorted. 'I wish. I was self-taught till I went to art school. I'd have loved to have learned sooner. I couldn't even take art at high school. My father didn't approve.'

'He didn't?'

Carissa shook her head and a tendril of hair escaped her severely pulled-back hairstyle. It flirted over her collarbone as if inviting his attention to the tight white top clinging to her breasts.

Her clothes reminded him that she wasn't as Alexei had first assumed. Instead of glamorous designer outfits from expensive shopping sprees, she favoured shorts and skirts, skimpy and incredibly sexy. And that black outfit, the leggings and loose T-shirt that didn't fit with the rest yet seemed right for a woman so obviously comfortable with her body and uninterested in primping.

Carissa didn't need fancy clothes to hold his attention. She was sexy, vehement, impulsive and had a mischievous sense of humour. She was full of energy and surprising depths.

And he wanted her more than he'd wanted anyone or anything in a long, long time. Perhaps ever.

Acknowledging it made something inside him still. As if the treadmill of his world, driving him on and on, paused, allowing him to take stock.

It was a strange sensation. As if he were an onlooker to his own life, his wants and needs.

And the result of that self-examination? The realisation that, after a lifetime of self-reliance, he wanted more. The laughter and sharing, the warmth of having someone special.

The revelation stopped Alexei's breath, crushed his lungs and made his heart thunder.

Share his life?

It shouldn't be a surprise. He had the example of his parents' loving partnership. Days ago he'd begun toying with the idea of finding someone to start a family with. But now the idea wasn't abstract. It wasn't a theoretical, faceless woman who came to mind.

It was one specific woman. One spirited, restful, infuriating, generous woman. A woman about whom he knew so little, yet felt he knew everything important.

Not that this was *love*.

Alexei wouldn't fall victim to sentimentality.

But Carissa and he shared more than sex. They'd exercised abstinence for days and he grew more, rather than less, interested. This warmth, respect and liking could form the foundation of a solid relationship.

Instead of rejecting the idea, he felt a quiver of anticipation. It was like the moment he'd realised his first software innovation really worked. That it had the makings of a runaway commercial success. He was a loner but deep down he'd always wanted more than solitude.

Alexei waited for common sense to kick in and object that he'd known Carissa just a week.

It stayed silent.

And all the while the effervescence in his blood signalled he was onto a winning idea.

He always trusted his instincts.

He stared at Carissa, absorbed in her drawing. She never tried to charm or flatter. It was refreshing not to be fussed over, to be treated as an equal, or, Alexei realised with a silent huff of laughter, as an inanimate object to be sketched. But he knew one touch, one word, even a *look*, would have her burning for him. She was her own woman, but she was his too.

For the moment.

Did he really want more?

If so, what about her father? Alexei couldn't let Carter off the hook.

She'd want nothing to do with Alexei once he brought her father to justice. Yet she knew that was Alexei's goal and it hadn't deterred her.

'Why didn't your father encourage you to study art?' Maybe father and daughter weren't as close as he'd imagined.

'He wanted me to do something useful. Like *economics*.' Mina's tone echoed horror. 'It would have been a disaster!'

That didn't sound like the man who'd spoken indulgently about his artistic daughter. But Carter had said she wasn't suited to business. Perhaps he'd originally wanted her to follow in his shoes. As for Carissa not coping with economics, Alexei recalled their conversations and knew she had a better-than-average understanding.

'So you persuaded your parents to let you try art.'

Her hand stopped on the page, her knuckles tightening. Had he hit a nerve?

'I didn't ask. I just applied.' Slowly her hand moved again, though her strokes weren't as bold as before. She stopped and raised her head. Alexei's curiosity rose as he saw her flushed cheeks.

'How about you?' Her bright eyes snared his and awareness throbbed. How easily they struck sparks. 'How did you start in IT? Did you spend all your free time as a kid on the computer?'

'Hardly. We didn't have one.'

He read the question in her expression yet she didn't ask. She kept to their unspoken agreement not to pry.

Alexei was the one pushing the boundaries. His curiosity was insatiable. He had to decide if he wanted more than the time they had left till the showdown with her father.

He needed to know more about this woman who engaged his mind as well as his body. To do that he'd have to share things he never shared with anyone. He paused, considering.

'There wasn't money when I was growing up, and what little we had my stepfather spent on himself.'

'He sounds unlikeable.'

'You could say that.' Alexei's vital organs knotted. 'He targeted my mother for the insurance money she inherited when my father died. It wasn't a fortune but it would have paid for a roof over our heads and a decent education for me.'

Instead the money had gone on his stepfather's whims. A sports car that he crashed while drunk.

A 'get rich quick' scheme that failed. Expensive clothes, 'business' expenses for unspecified enterprises that involved late-night entertaining.

'You didn't have a home or decent education?' He heard sympathy in Carissa's voice as she bent her head, concentrating on a new sketch. Of his hands clenched in fists rather than relaxed as before. There was something soothing, almost hypnotic about watching the lines appear on the page, seeing form appear out of what had seemed random scratchings.

Though she worked, he knew she focused on his words. There was a tension about her that hadn't been there earlier. But she didn't push. She gave him space, and a measure of privacy, avoiding his gaze.

'We had a roof for the first couple of years. Mum remortgaged the place to finance his spending but he ran through that soon enough. He lived off her for years but when the money went, so did he.'

Alexei raked a hand through his shaggy hair, then realised what he'd done.

'Sorry.' He dropped his hand, fisting it on his thigh like its mate.

'Don't worry.' Her upward look, with that fleeting smile, eased the old tension brewing inside. 'I'll sketch your hands however you hold them. I love them. I'm thinking of using them in a piece I want to do.'

Alexei scowled down at his tight hands. For reasons he couldn't define her words unsettled him. Love. She'd used the word casually, yet he'd experienced a pang of...could it be *yearning*?

It was easier, suddenly, to think about the past than the knotty issue of how she made him feel.

'He sounds despicable,' Carissa said, her quiet voice vibrating with rage. 'To target a woman. To *use* her. There are too many selfish people in the world.'

Alexei's stare sharpened. 'You sound like you've met some.' He'd imagined she'd led a cosseted life.

'A few.' Her mouth flattened and she flipped the page. 'Actually, can I move your hands?' Her eyes held his. Something passed between them that inexplicably loosened the tension in his shoulders.

'Sure.' He watched as she turned his hands so they lay, palms up and fingers cupped. Her own hands were narrow and warm. Alexei liked the brush of her fingers.

'You must have been relieved when your step-father left.'

'Definitely. He was a difficult man at the best of times and, believe me, there weren't many of those.' Alexei remembered the sound of his mother's sharp cry, waking him in the night. The hard crack of a beefy hand against his jaw and the lash of a belt around his backside. 'But the trouble didn't end when he went.'

'It didn't?' She lifted her head.

Alexei shrugged. 'He'd somehow run up debts in my mother's name, and loan sharks have no sympathy for defaulters.' Even if the defaulter was a defeated, desperate woman struggling to make ends meet. 'My mother worked three jobs to keep us safe from the enforcers.' Was it any wonder she'd worked herself into an early grave?

Warm fingers clasped his. Carissa didn't say anything but the gentle pressure was wonderfully soothing. Not that he needed sympathy. He'd conquered his past long ago. Yet he didn't move, just let her fingers curl around his, enjoying the sense of connection.

'That doesn't explain your education.'

'Sorry?'

'You indicated your education was patchy. Surely school was free.'

Alexei added tenaciousness to Carissa's qualities.

'I missed school to earn money to help out.'

'How old were you?' Her brow scrunched.

'Eleven. Early teens.'

Carissa shook her head and covered his cheek with her palm. The gesture felt like balm. How long had it been since anyone had tried to soothe his hurts? No one had since his mother. 'Your mother must have been so worried about you.'

Surprise jabbed him. But of course Carissa understood his mother's concern. After they'd stopped sniping at each other, he'd quickly recognised empathy as one of her core traits.

'She was, but I had to do my bit for the family.' There it was again. Family. Until this week he hadn't let himself think about how it had felt to be part of something bigger than himself. To care and be cared for.

'Having a mother to love you. That's special.'

'At least you and I were lucky enough to know our mothers.'

He frowned, registering Carissa's brittle smile and wistful eyes. Did she miss her mother? It wasn't long ago she'd died. 'I'm sorry, Carissa. Sorry for your loss.'

'Thank you.' She blinked, her eyes bright. Then she pulled her arm away and sat back.

Mina had no memories of her mother. She'd told herself that didn't matter. Her older sister, Ghizlan, had been as good as any mother, making up for their father's distance.

Yet Alexei's words reopened a raw wound. One she'd refused for years to recognise. She felt it now, the sharp pain of loneliness, of being rejected by her father, abandoned by the mother who'd died.

Self-pity was pathetic. She had Ghizlan and she couldn't wish for a better sister. And Huseyn, her brother-in-law, was a sweetie beneath that incredibly gruff exterior. She had her little niece and nephew in Jeirut, and there was her friend Carissa.

But no one just for her.

Mina hated the direction of her thoughts. *Look at Alexei.* He'd lost his father young and had all sorts of trouble as a kid but he didn't give in to self-pity.

'So how *did* you start in IT?'

'A community youth centre.' Alexei shook his

head. 'One of the staff was particularly persistent. I look back and realise how hard he worked even to get me to talk. But the place was heated and relatively safe so it appealed.'

'You weren't safe?' Silly to feel concern now. But Mina hated the idea of a young kid alone and scared.

Alexei shrugged. As usual, his shirt hung open over his broad chest and she watched the play of his muscles. It made her slightly dizzy. She wanted to plant her palm there, where his heart beat.

'It wasn't a good neighbourhood. There were gangs.' His tone was dismissive. 'And it didn't matter where we moved, the heavies collecting the money we owed always found us.'

We owed. Not his mother, or even his stepfather.

We.

Alexei had assumed responsibility for something that shouldn't have been his concern. He should have been running around a school playground without a care.

A lump rose in Mina's throat and she swallowed hard. Why was she so sentimental? Millions of children lived in harsh conditions they didn't deserve, some in her own country. She and

Ghizlan were particularly active in supporting disadvantaged children. But why did Alexei's past hurts specifically unsettle her?

Because you care for him.

You care too much.

'They had an old computer. One of the guys taught me and I discovered an aptitude for it.'

'You make it sound easy. You don't go from being a kid with a second-hand computer to launching a megasuccessful software and communications company.'

'True. But I won't bore you with a blow-by-blow description.'

Mina opened her mouth to protest. She was fascinated. She wanted to hear more about Alexei. Anything about him. But she sensed he'd had enough of the subject.

'How did they meet, your parents?'

His winged eyebrows lifted, giving him the look of a particularly rakish fallen angel, especially with that tousled hair threatening to flop over his forehead.

Fire ripped through her.

'Don't move a muscle.' She flipped a page and started drawing, trying to get the haughty angles, the stark beauty of spectacular cheekbones and determined jaw, the sensuality of his mouth.

As she worked, darting looks at him and then back to the paper, something changed. His expression grew less arrogant and more focused, the gleam in his eyes brighter. Mina became more than ever aware of Alexei's scent—cedar, citrus and male, with an undertone of musk. She inhaled deeply, her hand moving furiously across the paper. If Ghizlan could bottle that scent at her perfumery, the enterprise would make a fortune.

'Finished?' Those malachite eyes glinted more brightly than any faceted gem.

'Almost.' Mina read his impatience, sensed his arousal and strove for something to distract him. 'You didn't tell me how your parents met.'

'At the Olympics. He was an athlete and she was a physio travelling with the Russian team. They fell in love and eloped the day before the closing ceremony.'

'Wow! That's fast. They must have been head over heels.'

'They were. Completely and utterly in love. When my father died, my mother was devastated. It was almost too hard for her to go on.' His mouth twisted and Mina felt a thud of pain in her middle. 'That's why she remarried. She couldn't face the loneliness.'

Mina watched emotions play across Alexei's face. He looked angry, as if he blamed his mother. She'd made his life miserable with her rotten choice of second husband.

Yet things were rarely black and white. 'Maybe she wanted someone to take your father's place, for your sake. So you'd have a dad.'

The spasm of pain across his face lasted only a moment but it told her so much.

He felt guilty about his mother's choice?

And maybe for blaming her?

'How about you?' he asked. 'How did your parents meet?'

Mina felt a flutter in her chest. A battle between innate honesty and her need to cover for Carissa. Mina was increasingly uncomfortable with these lies. Surely Carissa was safe. The elopement was supposed to happen this weekend. She wanted so badly to blurt the truth but couldn't risk it.

Because you don't want this to end, do you? You want to stay here with Alexei and dream of impossible things.

She closed her sketchbook. She wouldn't give Carissa away, nor would she pretend to have lived Carissa's life.

'They didn't know each other before the engagement.'

'It was an arranged marriage?' He looked stunned.

'It's a tradition in my family.' Mina suppressed a pained smile. As far as she knew, her sister was the only woman in a long line of ancestors to find love in marriage. It wasn't something either of them had believed possible, having been bred as dynastic bargaining chips.

Now finding happiness with the man you loved, and who loved you, seemed incredibly alluring.

Mina put her sketchbook down, ignoring the drag of unhappiness. Her time with Alexei was limited. She refused to mar it. Instead she stood and stretched, forcing her attention away from *if onlys*.

'I've sat too long. I need exercise. How about another archery contest?' She'd been delighted to find it was a sport Alexei enjoyed, and one of the few she was proficient in, since it was Jeirut's national sport. 'Or a swim?' Her gaze turned towards the pristine beach. She'd had no qualms about using the brand-new swimsuit Carissa had packed. An errant thread of heat circled her womb at the thought of dispensing with the swimsuit and swimming naked with Alexei. If he knew the truth about her maybe they could...

Suddenly he was beside her. The fine hairs

on her arms and neck prickled and her insides melted.

'If it's exercise you want—' his voice was an earthy growl that tumbled down her backbone and drew her belly tight '—I know just the thing.' His green eyes darkened and she swayed towards him.

Then, abruptly, he stepped back and groaned, shaking his head. 'You'll be the death of me yet.' But his lips curved in a smile as he reached for her hand. 'Come on, we need to work off some of this surplus energy.' He tugged her hand and she followed.

That was the problem. She was long past resisting Alexei. She wanted to be with him, all the time.

She was headed for disaster and couldn't pull back.

CHAPTER THIRTEEN

PHONE TO HIS EAR, Alexei sat back in his desk chair, grinning. Ralph Carter had been found in a casino in southern Switzerland. Either through cunning or sheer luck, he'd led the investigators a merry dance, but now there was no escape. Carter would face the consequences of his theft.

Satisfaction warmed Alexei.

Until Carissa's face swam in his mind. He recalled her sparkling eyes, the throaty husk of her voice as she cried his name in ecstasy, her decadently addictive mouth.

How would she react when he made her father pay for his crimes?

Doubt stirred Alexei's gut. He'd learned this week that she was anything but a selfish social butterfly. He admired her honest, generous spirit, even her obstinacy. This would hurt her.

He stiffened his resolve. She couldn't expect him to forget her father's crime. She knew it was coming. She hadn't asked for mercy on Carter's behalf. Though now Alexei considered that odd, surely.

Carissa was passionate and unafraid of ruffling his feathers, yet she'd never tried to intercede for her father.

As he listened to his PA, Alexei reached idly for Carissa's sketchbook and flipped it open. She'd left it by the pool and he'd brought it inside when he took this call. Clearly she'd forgotten it, focused instead on the fact it was her turn to cook.

Tomorrow Henri and Marie returned and the food would be restaurant quality again. But Alexei would far rather have another week alone with Carissa, sharing responsibility for chores, than any amount of exquisite dishes.

His insides twisted. Alexei told himself it was from eagerness to face Carter. Not concern as he anticipated Carissa's reaction.

'Excellent. See to those arrangements and we'll wrap this up.'

'There's one more thing.' His PA sounded unexpectedly tentative. 'A woman has been ringing, insisting she speak with you.'

Alexei frowned. He paid his PA an excellent salary. In return he didn't expect to be bothered by importunate strangers. Obviously this woman was out of the ordinary. 'And?'

'She gave her name as Carissa Carter.'

Arrested, Alexei sat straighter. 'Say that again.'

'She claims to be Carissa Carter, daughter of Ralph Carter.'

Alexei looked at the sketch before him. It was one he hadn't seen before and there was something incredibly intimate about it. Not just the fact that he was asleep on a sun lounger. He felt tenderness in the way Carissa had drawn the rumpled hair shadowing his forehead, and the lines of his mouth.

Was that really how she saw him?

A curious buzz started up in his ears.

'Obviously the woman is lying.'

'That's what I thought. But she gave enough detail to be very convincing.'

The fact his PA pressed the point was significant. She was not only loyal but intelligent. She must have good reason for pursuing this. 'Very well. Give me her number.'

Minutes later Alexei made the call.

'Hello? Carissa speaking.' Her voice was high and breathy and slightly familiar.

Alexei leaned forward, hand splayed on the desk, pulse quickening.

'Carissa Carter?'

'Yes, I… Who is this?' Her voice wobbled and Alexei felt the blood drain from his face. He recognised the voice now. It was the woman he'd spoken to a week ago. The woman he'd arranged to have collected in Paris. He'd assumed the line had distorted her voice because she sounded different in person.

He pinched the bridge of his nose with his thumb and forefinger. 'It's Alexei Katsaros.'

He heard a gasp, then a noise as if she'd dropped the phone. Adrenalin shot through him and his stomach lurched.

'Are…are you there?'

'I'm here. What do you want?' The person responsible for this elaborate hoax would pay. Alexei was in no mood for games.

'I rang to tell you I got married. I know my father led you to believe I was…available but he was wrong. A match between us isn't possible.' Her words were rushed, her breathing so uneven the words slurred together. 'I should have told you my plans sooner. I'm sorry. But I was too… That is, I wasn't thinking clearly when you rang. Pierre said I should have told you straight, and so did Mina, but I was too…' She hiccupped as if holding back a sob. 'I've tried and tried to call Mina but I can't reach her. Is she all right?'

Alexei's head spun. His pulse throbbed so hard it felt like a hammer against his temple.

He wanted to tell this stranger to quit wasting his time. But something stopped him. The suspicion this was no joke. That the impossible was about to become possible.

Twenty minutes later Alexei stared unseeingly across his desk, the phone silenced.

He'd got to the bottom of the situation all right. He'd taken some convincing, and more checking, but he was absolutely sure the woman on the phone was Carissa Carter.

He reeled at learning the truth. All this time he'd thought his guest was his employee's daughter when she was Princess Mina of Jeirut, sister of the country's Queen. A rich royal who'd played the part of Carissa, duping him.

Making a fool of him.

Alexei imagined the field day the press would have with this. What impact would that have on his business? He screwed his eyes shut and tried to focus his scrambled brain on damage limitation.

But focus was impossible. It was all he could do to accept the preposterous truth. The two women had conned him. And he, so wrapped up in the pursuit of vengeance and the need to act decisively, had made it easy, not bothering to check details.

This wasn't business. It was far more personal. Briefly he acknowledged he'd made it so when he'd brought Carter's daughter to his private retreat. But his actions didn't sink to these depths of deception.

Alexei's gaze drifted to the abandoned sketchbook on his desk. He turned it over, opening it at the very beginning, to the images he hadn't viewed before. Why? Was he so desperate to believe, even now, that the woman in his kitchen was genuine? That the woman he'd come to care for was real, not some pretend persona adopted to dupe him?

Alexei stopped on the second page, on a series of intricate designs for a flask. They were exquisite. But it wasn't the design's beauty that caught his eye, it was the stylised calligraphy around the base. Calligraphy in Arabic. A talented artist could have copied the flowing script. Except there were also what looked like scribbled notes on the edge of the page in the same language.

Alexei turned the page. There was another bottle, again with scrawled notes in Arabic.

His mouth tightened. If he'd only taken the time to look, instead of being so caught up in that blaze of attraction for Carissa. For *Mina*, he corrected himself.

Despite Carissa Carter's breathless, half-defiant, half-apologetic explanations, Alexei knew they'd made a fool of him.

He looked down to see he'd again reached the page where she, *Mina*, had drawn him sleeping. With new eyes Alexei realised it wasn't tenderness revealed in the portrait. That wasn't vulnerability in his sleeping features but weakness. She'd been laughing at him.

She'd sashayed in, daring him to make a pass at her, teasing him till he didn't know which way was up. Pretending to be someone else, pretending to be honest and open and vulnerable. Had her virginity also been a lie?

Alexei shoved the book so hard it toppled off the desk as he surged to his feet and stalked to the window. It wasn't the view he saw. It was himself, laughing with… Mina. Telling Mina about his past, his stepfather, because he'd actually considered extending their relationship into something else.

Relationship!

He snorted. They had no relationship beyond sex and lies.

The sex he could cope with, but not the lies.

He'd been conned as a kid and that had brought disaster.

He'd trusted Carter, had actually liked him, believing he and the older man shared an understanding. Till Carter knifed him in the back and stole his money.

Now Alexei found himself tricked again. By a slip of a woman with big brown eyes and a devious mind. A woman who'd burrowed her way into his—

Alexei yanked his thoughts to safer ground. To the blaze of anger searing his gut.

She'd made him reconsider his single status. She'd made him think about babies and belonging and all the while...

He swore, a mix of Greek and Russian that was far more potent for cursing than English.

Only when he had himself under control did he turn towards the door.

Mina hummed as she took the casserole from the oven. The aromas were mouth-watering. This was the one meal she could cook well, a traditional spicy vegetable dish from her homeland. It had been worth the extra time and effort.

For once Mina would be able to present Alexei with something delicious. There was a spring in her step and a smile on her face as she crossed to put it on the counter.

Alexei never complained about her culinary efforts. Nor did she aim to become a domestic goddess. Yet there was something deeply satisfying about cooking something nice for your man.

Mina blinked, staring down at the fragrant meal in astonishment.

Your man. Where had that come from?

This was temporary. Alexei Katsaros wasn't her man and never would be. Yet some tremulous, defiant voice inside disagreed.

He *felt* like her man.

She *wanted* him to be hers.

Mina stumbled back against the big island bench and slumped there, her mind racing at the enormity of the revelation.

She crossed her arms over her chest as if she could contain the swelling sensation inside. The rising demand that she face the truth.

What she felt with Alexei was more profound than sexual attraction. She'd spent her time on the island studiously ignoring that, pretending this was animal magnetism and no more. Because the truth of what she felt was too enormous, too life-changing. Too preposterous.

She'd imagined herself immune to romance, to dreams of being with one special man. No one had come close to distracting her from her drive to make art. But Alexei did that, even though they hadn't had sex in days. No one had ever made her *feel*, made her want to be part of a couple.

Mina put her hand to her breastbone. Her heart pounded high and hard.

A noise on the other side of the room made her look up. Instantly the tightness in her chest eased, and something inside her soared.

Alexei stood in the doorway, one shoulder propped against the doorjamb, arms crossed over his chest in a way that accentuated the curves of well-developed biceps and pectorals.

Desire throbbed through her. And more, far more. When he was with her she no longer worried that she was out of her depth. With Alexei she felt utterly right. It should be crazy to feel this way after a mere week, but there was no avoiding her feelings.

Mina smiled, not bothering to hide her delight. 'Smells good, doesn't it?' She leaned over the dish, inhaling the aroma that reminded her of Jeirut. What would Alexei make of her homeland? She'd love to take him there. 'And I promise it's not charred or undercooked. I'll get the plates.'

'Surely you shouldn't be waiting on me, *Princess*.'

Mina's head jerked up as if yanked on a string. It wasn't just Alexei's words but his tone that shook her. She looked into that searing green gaze, registered the flaring nostrils and savagely flattened mouth. Her stomach plummeted.

He knew.

And he was livid.

Alexei watched the laughter and the blood drain from her face, leaving her features pale and proud.

In that moment his last hope that this was a mistake died. And with it the foolish desires he'd entertained.

He waited for her to show embarrassment or guilt. There would have been some satisfaction in that. He might even have listened to an explanation if she'd shown regret and shame.

Instead, she drew herself up, shoulders straight and pushed back. Her neck lengthened as her chin came up. The welcome in her eyes died, replaced with a hauteur Alexei recognised from her arrival on the island.

It was like watching an actress don another persona. Except instead of seeing a make-believe character, the woman confronting him with that cool stare and regal bearing *was* the real woman. A conniving, lying woman.

The enthusiastic, caring person he'd known was a chimera. She'd been created to hold his attention long enough to distract him from the fact he was being fooled. How much of her had been real? Any of it?

He slammed the lid on such thoughts. He refused to search for pitiful fragments of a woman who didn't exist beyond his imagination.

The anger that had been brewing since the phone calls bubbled over. 'You must be used to having servants scurrying to do everything.'

Her face changed even more, shutters coming down behind her eyes, making her unapproachable. No wonder he'd likened her to that Russian ballerina. Both could project regal hauteur fit for a queen.

But no blue-blooded princess would play a part for public entertainment like a dancer. How much had her role-playing been for personal entertainment? Had she laughed at how easily she'd fooled him?

A knife twisted in his chest.

'You're wrong, Alexei. I have no servants.'

Maybe it was the way she said his name, her voice husky and low, reminding him of her throaty purrs as she climaxed, that fuelled his ire to spilling point. More probably it was the unblinking gaze that revealed the barriers she erected between herself and the hoi polloi.

After all, despite his wealth, Alexei had spent most of his early years living in slums. Whereas she was descended from generations of royalty.

This was the woman he'd wanted in his bed, his home, his life. She'd laugh if she knew exactly how much of a fool she'd made him.

'Quit lying, Princess. The pretence is over.'

He spoke like a stranger. A looming, ice-cold stranger. Shock made Mina shuffle back a step.

If there was ever a time to call on those early lessons in self-control, this was it. This furious stranger wasn't her lover. She knew without question this man wouldn't respond to appeals for mercy or reason. He had no softer side.

Mina had known there'd be trouble when the truth emerged. But lately she'd convinced herself it wouldn't be so bad. Maybe she and Alexei might even laugh it off.

Only sheer willpower stifled the hysterical laughter bubbling inside. Again she'd been naive.

Desperately she wrapped herself tighter in that cloak of composure she'd learned to wear since childhood. The cloak she'd worn when facing her father's beetling regard, or the curious stares of the public. Both had been more concerned with the appearance of royalty than the real girl behind the façade.

'You're right.' She breathed deep. 'It's time for the truth.' With every hour she'd sunk deeper into that hazy world of self-deception, where Alexei cared for her as much as she did him.

'Past time.' He spoke through gritted teeth. 'You *are* Princess Mina of Jeirut, aren't you?' He said it as if it were a mark of shame rather than honour.

Wearily Mina nodded. 'I am.' She searched for what to say next, then surprised herself by blurting out, 'But it's true. I don't have servants. I look after myself.'

Why she insisted on telling him, she didn't know. His expression showed he wasn't interested. Yet it seemed important he understand she was an ordinary person despite her lineage.

'Is that a ploy for sympathy?' His eyebrows rose mockingly. 'Did you do this scam for money? Because you've spent your inheritance?' His words bit so deep it was a wonder they didn't leave marks. 'Are you looking for someone to fund your lifestyle?'

The insult wasn't camouflaged. Even someone as inexperienced as she could read the curl of his lip and the dismissive gaze flicking her from face to feet.

Something inside Mina shrivelled, like a delicate bloom blasted by the desert sun. The ache inside became a tearing pain but she wouldn't let it show. 'Don't be ridiculous. I——'

'Ridiculous?' He straightened from the doorjamb and prowled towards her, arms still crossed. He didn't stop till he was right in front of her, toe to toe.

Mina blinked and widened her stance, grounding herself rather than stepping back. He intimidated her. If she weren't shell-shocked by his reaction she'd probably be scared. But pride refused to let her reveal that.

'Of course it's ridiculous. I'm not after financial support.' How could he believe that? Did he think everyone was out for what they could get from him?

'Then what was this past week? Some social experiment for a cosseted princess to see how the other half lives? Was royal life so tame you wanted to spice it up with someone who grew up on the other side of the tracks?'

Horror stole her voice for precious seconds. 'You can't believe that!' It was a scratchy whisper.

'Why not?' He leaned close and Mina read nothing but contempt in his eyes.

'I'd hardly call a man with your power and finances anyone's idea of a bit of rough.' How dared he attack *her*? Yes, she was culpable. She'd lied and she hadn't been comfortable with it but she'd had good reason. 'Secondly, you need to take responsibility for what happened.'

'Me?' He had the nerve to look outraged.

'Who else?' Through the pain anger erupted. 'You put Carissa through hell. And I—'

'You what? You can't tell me this last week has been your idea of hell.' He leaned in and Mina inhaled the cedar-and-citrus scent that always made her senses tingle. To her horror she felt a softening between her thighs, as if, even facing Alexei's scorn, she wanted him.

She drew herself up, slowly reciting in her head

the names of her five favourite sculptors, then another five, till she trusted her voice.

'I did what I did for my friend. You threatened to kidnap her.'

'I did no such thing. Her father offered her to me and I simply invited her here to—'

'Rubbish!' Mina's control frayed and she prodded her fingers into the solid muscle of his shoulder. '*You* started this when you decided to use Carissa for your own ends. Have you any idea how scared she was when she got your call?'

'Because she was in cahoots with her father.' If possible he looked even grimmer than before.

Mina shook her head. 'If you knew Carissa you'd know that was impossible. She can't tell a lie to save herself. She couldn't even think of an excuse to fob you off when you sent your goons to collect her.'

'But it wasn't Carissa who came, was it? It was you, lying through your teeth.'

'You expect me to apologise for that?' The nerve of the man stupefied her. 'I've known some manipulative men. Men who'd use a woman as a convenience as if she weren't a real person. But I thought they were dying out. Until I met you.'

Mina refused to think about the man she'd

fallen for this past week. He'd either been a mirage invented by her yearning soul or a cruel joke.

'You brought this on yourself. Poor Carissa was beside herself, thinking her father would lose his job unless she agreed to come.'

Mina stepped back, not in retreat but so she could turn and march across the kitchen. She couldn't stay still, couldn't pretend to be calm. Not when everything had gone up in flames.

'Don't you walk away from me!' The growl came from just behind her and the hairs at her nape stood to attention.

'Or what?' She spun round and fixed her tormentor with a furious stare, barely able to believe how this confrontation had exploded. 'You'll lock me up? Hold me to ransom?'

'You're so sure your royal status exempts you from the consequences of your actions.'

'This has nothing to do with being royal.'

Alexei's eyes blazed. 'You deliberately connived to keep me from finding Carter. The man's a thief.'

'*All* I did—' she jammed her hands on her hips '—was buy time so my friend wouldn't be railroaded into marrying an arrogant jerk who treats people like disposable toys.' Mina drew a deep breath. 'Did you ever, once, stop to consider the collateral damage to other people from your actions?'

'Like you, I presume? You're claiming to be an injured party?' His contemptuous stare incinerated her last, frail hope. 'I'm no expert on Jeirut but I know it's very traditional. A royal princess who has casual flings would be frowned on. What's your plan? To claim I forced you into my bed when it comes out we've been alone for days?' His voice was a snarl, ripping through her stupid fantasies.

'How can you think such a thing?' Tears of indignation and pain needled the backs of her eyes.

His eyebrows lifted, the only sign of animation in a face turned mask-like.

'Then what? A kiss-and-tell story for the media? You'd get a small fortune for that, and revenge for your friend. But you'd wreck your reputation at home if it came out you had an affair.' He paused, his mouth tightening. 'Or am I to expect a demand from the King of Jeirut that I pay for the privilege of having despoiled your supposed virginal status?'

Mina flinched at his brutal accusations. How could he *think* such things? A yawning pit of hurt opened up inside.

'I see.' Abruptly Alexei's fury vanished, re-

placed by a look of weariness and bitter disillu-
sionment. His voice turned flat. 'So that's it. You
have your bit of fun and expect someone else to
pay the price.'

Mina opened her mouth and shut it again. She
was without words. How had she given her heart
to a man who thought so little of her? For it was
her heart she'd lost to Alexei, not just her innocence.

She pressed her hand to her middle, trying to
hold in the lacerating anguish that felt as if her
insides had crystallised to glass and shattered.
She'd gone from heady delight to the depths of
humiliation and pain so fast her head spun.

She needed to find words to make him understand. But what was the point? This wasn't her
Alexei. This was a man who could believe the
absolute worst of her. Her Alexei was nothing
but a phantom.

'I'd like to leave the island now.' Her voice was
stilted but she was beyond caring. 'I assume you
can arrange that?'

'Nothing would give me greater pleasure.'

Mina turned to the door, unable to face his disdain any longer. 'Excellent. At least that's one
thing we agree on.'

CHAPTER FOURTEEN

PARIS WASN'T FAR enough away.

Mina stared at the blinking light of her message bank and knew if she hit Play, Alexei's deep voice would fill the room. Worse, it would inveigle its way inside her, reinforcing the hollow ache she carried.

She knew because that was what had happened earlier. She'd come out of the shower and hadn't thought twice about checking her messages. Only to find herself fighting a rush of pain at the sound of that familiar voice. She'd slammed the phone down and deleted his message, unable to listen.

It didn't matter if he'd rung to berate her some more, or even to apologise for his sniping accusations. The fact was she *had* lied to him. But worse, she'd made the mistake of falling for the man.

Even if he called to say he was sorry he overreacted, which was about as likely as snowfall in the desert, it wouldn't be enough. Even if by some miracle he'd forgiven her and decided the sex between them was so good he wanted an affair, Mina knew she needed more.

She needed all or nothing.

Nothing was the only logical option.

Mina turned and paced. She needed space to think. Somewhere with no reminders of him.

A tattoo on the front door made her heart leap. It couldn't be. She didn't want it to be. Yet her hands shook as she opened it. Savage disappointment sliced through her at the sight of her best friend.

Mina really was desperate. And delusional. As if Alexei would turn up at her door!

'Carissa!'

Her friend enveloped her in a hug and a cloud of rose perfume. 'Are you okay? You look like hell.'

Mina managed a chuckle, despite the scratchy throat that made it hard to swallow. 'Lack of sleep. I'll be fine. But you look fabulous. Marriage agrees with you.'

Carissa grinned. She'd never looked prettier. Something tugged at Mina's heart but she refused to feel jealous that her friend had found happiness with the man she adored.

'It *is* wonderful. Pierre's the best. And I have you to thank. Without you stepping in—'

'I was glad to help.' Mina shut the door and led her towards the lounge room. But Carissa stopped her.

'I'm sorry, sweetie. I don't have time. Pierre and I are heading off to see his family. He's going to introduce me, so wish us luck.'

'They'll love you once they get to know you.' Mina pressed her hands. 'Give them a little time.'

Carissa nodded. 'That's what Pierre said. But I'm not sure and—' Her eyes rounded. 'How could I forget? Are you in trouble? That's what I came to ask.'

'Trouble?'

Carissa nodded. 'You must have got home very late last night. I didn't even know you were back. Then just now I was coming up the street when I saw those men. The ones who took you to Alexei Katsaros. They were coming out of our building and drove away in a big black car.'

'You're sure it was them?' Had she missed a knock on the door as she dried her hair?

Emotions stormed through Mina. Excitement vied with hope that she knew she had to crush. She and Alexei had no future.

'As if I'd forget.' Carissa shivered. 'I got a good look through the peephole the day they took you away. What do they want? Why are they here?'

'Probably checking I got home safely.' Maybe Alexei's conscience was troubling him and he wanted to make sure. Last night she'd refused an escort from the airport, insisting on finding her own way home.

'You're such a bad liar, Mina. I'll tell Pierre we can't go yet—'

'No. You have to go.' Her words were sharp, yet her mouth quivered. Reaction, she told herself. She'd barely slept. She needed time alone.

'Then what can I do to help?' Carissa put her arm around her and Mina had to fight the urge to weep on her shoulder.

Mina never ran from trouble but she felt too raw, too destroyed by the enormity of her feelings to cope. She needed to lick her wounds and recoup. 'Help me pack a bag. I'm going to Jeirut.'

The royal palace of Jeirut was imposing and war-like. Only the banners snapping in the wind alleviated its grimness. Perched on a high plateau, it commanded views of the city spread around it and the desert below.

Alexei followed a courtier through an oversized portal into a series of antechambers, each more magnificent than the last. But Alexei wasn't in the mood to be impressed. His mind was on the upcoming interview.

His one chance. The knowledge tightened his gut.

Finally he was led into an audience chamber with a forest of pillars around the perimeter. His gaze went to the golden throne and on it a tall, powerfully built man in white robes. His face was rugged, his nose uneven and eyes piercing. This man—Alexei knew, his pulse quickening in anticipation—made even the best negotiators nervous.

Introductions were made, complete with a scraping bow from Alexei's companion. Sheikh Huseyn, colloquially known as the Iron Hand, remained stony-faced. It was only when the doors closed behind the courtier and Alexei was alone with Mina's brother-in-law that the Sheikh raised one eyebrow in interrogation.

'You have a request?'

Alexei met that assessing stare with one of his own. 'I want to speak with your sister-in-law.' As if Sheikh Huseyn didn't already know that. As if Alexei hadn't been through this multiple times with officials.

'If you have something important to say, I can pass on a message. At present she's busy.'

Alexei wasn't deterred. He'd missed her in Paris but he *would* see her here. Mina might be furious and hurt but she wouldn't hide from him. She was too proud.

At least he hoped so. Unless he'd given her such a disgust of him that even her pride wasn't enough. He shoved the idea aside, refusing to countenance the idea of defeat.

'Thank you. But I prefer to speak with Mina.'

Sheikh Huseyn's eyes narrowed as if questioning his use of Mina's name.

'Why should I let you see her?' His even tone held an undercurrent of menace.

Instead of being abashed, Alexei stepped closer. Royalty or not, he refused to let the Sheikh stand in his way. 'Surely that's Mina's decision.'

The Sheikh didn't reply and as the silence lengthened, ice-cold sweat trickled down Alexei's spine.

'Are you saying Mina refuses to see me?' Nausea rolled through him. He tasted acid and recognised it as fear. Would Mina send him away without a chance?

'Why should she? What's your relationship?'

'That's between me and Mina.' Alexei's gaze followed the perimeter of the room. Did one of those doors lead to her? Frustration rose. The palace was enormous. If he made a break for it he had no hope of finding her before the royal guard stopped him.

'And if I make it my business?' The Sheikh rose and stepped onto the floor. He moved with the ease of an athlete and, sizing him up, Alexei guessed they'd be well matched in a tussle.

'I can only repeat that my business is solely with Mina.'

'I am her King and head of her family.' Huseyn moved to stand toe to toe with Alexei. The air was redolent with latent danger. 'It's my role to protect her.'

Alexei met his eyes. 'I respect your desire to protect her, but Mina can manage her own concerns. I doubt she'd be impressed by anyone, even family, speaking on her behalf.'

A ripple of expression crossed the Sheikh's features, then, to Alexei's surprise, his face creased in a smile.

'You know Mina well.' He paused. 'What brings you to Jeirut? Surely not simply seeing my sister-in-law. Are you opening an office here? Or perhaps one of your youth centres. Such a laudable programme.'

Huseyn had done his homework. Alexei respected that. It was what he would have done. Due diligence was second nature.

Except that one vital time when he hadn't checked out Carissa Carter because he'd been determined to snaffle her quickly as bait. Technically that had been a grave error, but Alexei couldn't think of it in those terms since it had brought him Mina.

Elusive Mina. He stifled impatience with difficulty.

'I congratulate you, Highness. Not many know of my link to that initiative.' Alexei made sure of it. His community training and support scheme for disadvantaged teenagers wasn't done for kudos but to make a difference. Those kids didn't need their problems aired for public sympathy when Alexei could quietly provide the start-up money for programmes that eventually became self-funding.

'I make it my business to know about men who take an interest in my sister-in-law.'

Huseyn was toying with him. Mina had been a sexual innocent until she'd come to him. Despite what he'd thought in the white-hot sear of anger.

'So, would you be interested in working in Jeirut?'

'It depends on the result of my discussion with

Mina.' Alexei set his jaw. 'Is that the price for letting me see her?'

For a moment longer the Sheikh watched him through narrowed eyes. Then he nodded abruptly as if coming to a decision. 'You're not what I expected, Mr Katsaros.' He paused. 'Come, I'll take you to her.'

So he'd passed a test. Alexei should have felt relieved. Instead, as he followed Huseyn he felt more nervous than he could ever remember.

Perhaps that was why, when the Sheikh ushered him into a lavish chamber, it took Alexei a moment to recognise Mina. There were two women, both focused on a velvet-lined jewellery case open on a table. One he knew from his research as the beautiful Sheikha of Jeirut. The other... His breath stopped as she looked up and eyes of rich brown snared his.

Mina. One look and the ground shuddered beneath his feet. Yearning filled him.

Instead of the casual clothes he was accustomed to, she wore an evening dress of crimson with a square-cut neckline that emphasised the purity of her slender throat and graceful posture. Her hair was up and a tiara of brilliant diamonds sparkled in that dark mass.

How had he ever imagined her to be Carissa Carter? She was every inch a princess.

She was the most stunning woman he'd ever beheld.

Alexei's heart battered his ribs as he fought not to cross the room and pull her close.

As he watched her mouth flattened into a straight line and her beautiful eyes clouded. The hurt he saw there tore his conscience and his hopes.

All his resolve, all his certainty he could set things right, were shaken to the core.

He looked the same. No, not the same. Bigger, sexier, more charismatic than she'd let herself remember.

Heat swamped Mina. Her quiver of awareness was proof that, if anything, memory had done Alexei Katsaros a disservice. The only change in him, apart from the suave suit, was that he looked hollow around the eyes. Tired from travel. She wouldn't allow herself to imagine their parting had interfered with his sleep.

She was the one cursed with wakeful nights.

She drew a deep breath, hands clenching. That was when she remembered the diamond necklace in her palm. She moved to put it in its box but her hand shook ridiculously. Fortunately Ghizlan reached out and scooped it from her.

Mina had been on tenterhooks all day, unable to settle, after Huseyn told her Alexei was coming. Ghizlan's insistence that she decide on some finery for an upcoming royal reception had been a welcome diversion that stopped her checking the time every two minutes.

Now she'd been caught all glammed up. Full-length silk rustled as she shifted. Diamond drops swung from her earlobes and she was conscious of the pins securing the heirloom tiara.

Her chin tilted as she took in Alexei's stare. So what if he had a problem with her royal status? She wasn't ashamed. She was what she was, as much at home in a formal gown as old jeans.

'Mina.' Alexei's voice was the same, a deep cadence that did crazy things to her self-control.

She drew a sustaining breath. 'Alexei.' Then she turned to her sister. 'Ghizlan, this is Mr Katsaros.'

'Mr Katsaros.' Contrary to her usual friendly manner, Ghizlan gave the tiniest nod, her expression a degree short of glacial.

Alexei didn't look fazed by the lack of welcome. 'Your Highness.' His eyes tracked back to Mina.

She'd arrived here unexpectedly, desperate for the comfort of her sister's presence. Like when she'd been a child. Ghizlan and Huseyn had, in their different ways, provided that comfort. Huseyn's expression now made it clear he'd intervene if Alexei upset Mina, and Ghizlan bristled with protectiveness. She'd guessed Alexei had caused the unhappiness Mina couldn't hide. Bless her, and Huseyn too, for closing ranks.

But this was Mina's battle.

'I'd like to speak to Alexei alone.' It was a lie. Facing him was torment. But this had to be done. One final conversation and their abortive relationship would be over. Pain crested to a point behind her ribs and Mina rubbed the spot, till Alexei tracked the movement. She dropped her hand.

Huseyn folded his arms. 'Anything he wishes to say can be said before your family.'

'But surely,' Alexei said, without taking his eyes from her, 'Mina has the right to privacy.'

Mina stifled the urge to roll her eyes. The air was thick with testosterone, the two very alpha males each determined to stand their ground.

'This won't take long.' Mina ignored the pang of regret she felt at that, and sent a pleading glance to Ghizlan. 'Then I'll come and join you.'

After a searching glance Ghizlan nodded. 'We'll finish this later.' Not just the choice of jewels, but, she made clear, a conversation about Alexei Katsaros.

Wearily Mina nodded. She owed Ghizlan an explanation even if it was a truncated version of the truth. For no matter how she'd tried, since arriving in Jeirut she hadn't been able to hide the fact that something was terribly wrong.

Her sister took Huseyn's arm. For a moment he stood, unmoving. Then he nodded. 'Very well. We'll be in my study.' His tone held a warning as if daring Alexei to step out of line.

'Your family is very protective,' he said when the door closed.

'They are.' Sometimes overprotective. But there was comfort in having family who cared.

'I'm glad. You deserve to have people who care.'

Surprised, she shot Alexei a wary glance and was snared by those green eyes she'd tried to avoid.

It was impossible to look away, no matter how she ordered herself to do so. It was as if he drew her to him, compelled her against her will.

No, not against her will. That was the problem. Despite everything, Mina couldn't eradicate her weakness for Alexei. All she could do was pretend it didn't exist. It *shouldn't* exist. They'd only been together for a week. Far too short a time to fall in love. What she felt was infatuation.

A lump rose in her throat as she fought to stifle her feelings. She felt so wretched, not like herself at all. Once she'd have lost herself in work no matter what was going on around her. Now work took second place to the pain she carried like a layer beneath her skin.

Mina propped her hands on the table, grateful for something to lean on. She hadn't thought he'd come. Whenever she thought of that last day his words burned her soul. She'd told herself he'd spoken in the heat of the moment. That he didn't really believe what he'd said. But maybe he had.

After days of thinking herself at her lowest possible ebb, Mina knew she'd finally hit rock bottom. Shame, outrage and, yes, sheer hurt, scraped every inch of her flesh, making it smart. She tore her gaze away, pretending to tidy the gems that blurred before her eyes.

'I know because you're standing there, unscathed, you didn't suggest to Huseyn that you owed him a fee for taking my virginity.' She spat the words out, hating their acid taste. 'So let me reiterate, once and for all, I don't need your wealth. Nor does my family. There's no fine to pay.'

In the old days it would have been called a bride price and the suitor would have been ushered into a hasty marriage. But Alexei was no suitor. He despised her.

Mina clasped her hands, projecting as much calm as she could when her heart pounded like the hoofs of a runaway stallion. 'So there's no reason for you to stay. I can arrange for you to be on the next flight out.'

'I didn't come for that, Mina.'

His voice didn't sound right. She was used to lazy cadences, the mellifluous sound of a man confident and at ease. Her senses quickened at that too-tight timbre, as if something squeezed his voice box. Till his meaning sank in.

There was only one other reason for Alexei to come.

Another scrape of pain, this time so deep Mina was surprised she didn't see blood.

She lifted her head and met his eyes. The shock of what she saw reverberated through her. He looked gaunt and strained where minutes ago he'd looked solid and strong. His olive complexion was a sickly grey that made his eyes look sunken.

The alteration was so profound she actually moved towards him, then stopped mid-step.

'If you've come to check if I'm pregnant, you can relax.' Her voice was harsh. 'Those condoms did the trick. No inconvenient accidents to worry about.'

To her surprise Alexei recoiled as if from the lash of a whip.

'Are you sure?' His voice held a husky quality that reminded her too much of his words of praise and encouragement when they'd made lo—when they'd had sex. 'I assumed your supposed period was a sham.'

Mina's fingers pressed tight together. 'Absolutely sure.'

She'd been amazed to find herself fighting tears when she arrived in Paris and discovered her period really had started. She should have been relieved, she *was* relieved there was no pregnancy to complicate things. Yet it had been final confirmation that the fantasy was over.

'I'm sorry, Mina.'

She blinked and realised he'd closed the space between them. Instantly she stiffened. 'Sorry there's no baby? I can't believe that.'

'Sorry for *everything*.' He lifted both hands in a gesture that was at once open and weary, as if he carried an impossibly heavy weight. 'If I could eradicate everything I said that day I would. I'm *ashamed* of the accusations I threw at you. That's why I came, to apologise.'

Mina stared, grappling to connect this desperate man with the one she recognised. They were both Alexei, both real, but this one, with the anguished eyes, was new.

'You were right, Mina. I need to take responsibility for my actions. Instead I got wrapped up in my disappointment.'

'Disappointment?' At last she found her voice. 'It was more than that. It was rage.'

He inclined his head, but paused as if gathering himself. His mouth lifted in a bitter curve.

'You probably won't believe this, but I'm renowned for never losing my cool, even when things go badly wrong, even in highly pressured situations. I don't waste energy on anger because I prefer to focus on fixing things and moving on.'

Mina opened her mouth to argue when Alexei put up his hand. 'Please, hear me out.' Reluctantly she nodded and watched as he drew a breath that expanded his chest mightily. He looked intimidatingly big and bold and heartbreakingly desirable, yet his expression indicated a pain that might even match her own. She didn't understand what he wanted but she had to hear him out.

His hands dropped. 'As a kid I had a lot of anger, directed at my stepfather. Then at the people who harried my mother into an early grave. But I learned to control my feelings and focus on the future. It worked. Once I had that goal I had somewhere to channel my energies.'

Alexei waved an impatient hand. 'Sorry. Too much information.'

Mina was fascinated. But she was desperate to discover why he'd come. 'Get to the point, Alexei.'

A brief smile curled his lips but it wasn't reflected in his eyes. 'The point is I never lose control. Only twice. First when I discovered Ralph Carter had swindled the company and betrayed me.' His voice dropped to a sombre note. 'I'd trusted him, you see. The first person I'd actually trusted in...' He waved a dismissive hand again. 'Not that it matters.'

It mattered. It didn't take an expert to understand Alexei had major trust issues.

'Then, when I realised you weren't who you said, I lost it. Totally.' He shook his head and the lock of dark hair that had been combed back ruthlessly from his forehead tumbled over his brow, reminding her of the rumpled, gorgeous beachcomber she'd known in the Caribbean.

Brilliant green eyes focused on Mina. 'I told myself I was furious because you'd fooled me, that you and Carissa were laughing at me. I know now you weren't. But at the time all I could feel was hurt that I'd believed in you, *trusted* you and you'd betrayed that trust.'

There was that word again.

Alexei stood straighter. 'I lashed out because I cared for you, Mina. I wanted more from you than I'd ever wanted with anyone else. That's why I was furious. Because I hoped...' He stopped and she leaned forward, eager for more. 'As I said, it doesn't excuse my behaviour. You didn't deserve that and I apologise.'

Mina stared, trying to read his thoughts. She saw regret and shame. But what else?

'What did you hope, Alexei?' Her nerves were shredded, her heart racing.

Those stunning, familiar eyes locked on hers. 'I'd hoped we might have a future together.' His voice dropped. 'I'd even wondered how you felt about children.'

Mina gaped at him. 'But we'd only known each other a week.'

He shrugged, the usually fluid movement jerky.

'I trust my instinct. A week was long enough for me to feel things I've never felt before.'

'Things?' Her breath was a shallow draught of oxygen scented with warm male. Her brain froze.

Large hands took hers, their touch gentle yet compelling.

'Emotions. Not just desire but affection. Trust. Pride. Caring.' His eyes clouded. 'Not that you'd think so, the way I went for you when the truth came out.' His hands tightened on hers. 'The way I overreacted has nagged at me ever since.'

Mina watched him swallow. 'It made me realise the way I've stifled my emotions all these years isn't healthy. I'm determined to learn a better way to deal with my feelings. I need to make changes.'

Mina stared into Alexei's determined features, her emotions splintering in a dozen directions.

Wonder that he was here, baring his soul.

Sadness that his childhood experiences had affected him so profoundly.

Pride that he should confront his problems head-on and take action. Most men would run a mile from the idea of examining emotions and their own behaviour.

Regret that Alexei took all the blame when there'd been fault on both sides.

But above all excitement that he was here because he cared for her. He'd wondered about the future…with her! Did he still wonder? Or was he here simply to explain? Surely he couldn't be so cruel.

'I'm sorry too, Alexei. I lied to you and I wasn't comfortable about it—'

'You were protecting your friend.' His hands squeezed hers. 'Loyalty like that is a wonderful thing.'

'Even if I acted impulsively?' Her eyebrows rose.

'If you hadn't, we wouldn't have met.'

The look he gave her, grave yet intense, turned her heart over. No man had looked at her that way. As if he spoke to *her*. Not the artist or the princess but the woman who sometimes struggled to find her way, who loved her life, yet made mistakes and sometimes doubted herself, like everyone else.

'You're not saying anything.' His hands tightened.

'We both overreacted.' Mina drew a shuddery breath as if she'd inhaled a field full of butterflies. 'I was so attracted to you but scared of what I felt.' Even though it was glorious it was far beyond her experience.

Was that why she'd given up so easily, scurrying away rather than forcing him to accept the truth? Because she was frightened of where such a relationship might lead? Because she was used to being alone, not trusting anyone to know her fully?

'Was? In the past?' His voice was harsh, cracking on the last word.

Mina stared into that proud, handsome face, drinking in the familiar features that could seem intimidating or playful and right now looked drawn with tension.

She tilted her face high, defying the cowardly impulse to lie. 'Am. Right now.' It felt like the bravest thing she'd ever done, admitting that.

Mina swallowed as he stroked the line of her jaw from ear to chin.

'Me, as well. I'm attracted and scared too.'

Her lips curved in an unsteady smile. 'Who are you and what have you done with Alexei Katsaros? He's not scared of anything.'

He shook his head. 'I'm scared of losing you. Scared I blew my chance.' His words made everything within her still.

'Your chance for an affair?' She had to ask, though she knew, deep inside, what he meant. She needed the words.

Alexei cupped her face in both hands, leaning in so his words feathered her mouth. 'My chance to build a future with you. I know it's too early. I know we barely know each other, but there's something about you, Mina, that I can't do without. I want you in my life and I'll do whatever I must to convince you to give me that chance.' He drew a deep breath and she felt his hands shake. 'I think I'm in love with you.'

His words resonated like the echo of a bell, the sound filling her with not just joy, but recognition.

'It's unsettling, isn't it?'

For a moment Alexei looked dumbfounded, as if he couldn't believe his ears. Then his face creased into a smile so broad it blinded. He released her hands and instead wrapped his arms around her, yanking her close so she was pressed against his hot, hard frame. It was heaven. Mina melted into him, her hands clutching, wearing a grin of her own.

Was this really happening?

'Unsettling in the best possible way.' He paused, his eyes locked on hers so Mina felt as if she were falling into a deep, bright sea. 'You mean that? You feel—'

'I've been falling in love with you since the

day I reached your island and you made me furious and turned on at the same time.' Mina shook her head. 'I thought love was supposed to be all hearts and roses but you make me feel—' she struggled for words to convey at least some of her feelings '—*everything.*'

He nodded, his smile fading, eyes serious. 'Exactly. I want you even when we're arguing. Even when we don't agree. I want to make love to you all the time, but I also simply want to be with you, to share with you. To grow together.'

'Even though I live in Paris and you live—'

'I'm flexible. I can move.'

Mina's eyebrows shot up. He was a CEO with a business to run. She was the artist who could work almost anywhere. 'Even though I'm a princess?'

'You're not getting away from me that easily.' He lifted a hand to her hair and began to tug out the pins that secured it up. 'Besides, you look hot in a tiara.'

Mina saw a devilish glint in his eyes and sweet heat pierced her middle.

'Even though my best friend is Ralph Carter's daughter?'

Alexei shook his head. 'Stop trying to distract me. It won't work.'

'Distract you?'

Alexei's face lowered till his lips almost touched hers. 'I'm going to kiss you, Mina, till you stop throwing up objections. I'm going to kiss you till you agree to let me into your life so I can prove how good we'll be together.' All tension was gone from his face, replaced with a smug determination that made Mina want to laugh. For the first time today he looked like the man she'd fallen in love with.

For the first time since she left the Caribbean she felt happy.

'And if I don't agree?'

'Then, my sweet, sexy, Princess, I'll have to keep kissing you till you do.' There he was again, the confident tycoon with lurking humour in those slumberous eyes. But the tension humming through him, and the racing flick of the pulse at his temple, revealed Alexei took nothing for granted. He was still tense, waiting.

That, most of all, showed the change in him.

His lips brushed hers and Mina's knees went weak. Her arms tightened around his neck.

'If I agree, we need to take things slowly, get to know each other properly. We barely know each other.'

'I believe we know each other in the ways that

count.' Alexei nuzzled the base of her throat and delight shuddered through her. 'But I won't rush you.'

'I should warn you, I'm no pushover.' Yet she arched against him.

Alexei lifted his head, his smile wickedly knowing. 'I'm counting on it. I'm here for the long haul.' Then he took her mouth with his and Mina entered a world of bliss.

Ages later she heard a man clear his throat. Huseyn. It had to be. But Alexei didn't react and Mina was too lost in a haze of delight to pull back.

Her brother-in-law wasn't used to being ignored. Would he march over and pull them apart? Then she heard Ghizlan murmur something and the door clicked shut.

Alexei pulled back enough to look down at her. The gleam in his eyes made her heart tumble. 'So, your family is tactful as well as protective? I like them better all the time.'

Mina dragged air into starved lungs. 'Don't think they'll make it easy for you. They'll give you the third degree about your life, goals and intentions.'

His smiling eyes held hers. 'I can't think of anything else I'd rather discuss.' He stepped back the tiniest fraction, unhooking one of her hands from his neck and bringing it to his lips. 'My intention is to be the man who'll make you happy. Always.'

EPILOGUE

A YEAR LATER, to the day, Alexei entered their Parisian home. Not the cramped place Mina had rented, but a spacious, high-ceilinged house with space for a studio. He smiled. That was where she'd be, working, even though there was barely time for him to shower and change before they headed to tonight's exhibition.

He ripped off the tie he'd worn for a press conference and tossed it over the back of a settee. His pulse quickened as he headed for the studio. Thinking of Mina filled him with a heady excitement he didn't think would ever fade.

But for once his sweetheart wasn't up to her elbows in clay or working with metal. The place was empty, save for the usual clutter. A half-finished piece stood near the window. Sketches were pinned to one wall near a scuffed workbench.

Alexei's eyes went to a small, familiar piece in bronze on a nearby table. A man's hands, *his* hands, cupped and holding the slim fingers of a woman. *Mina's*. Though he appeared to support her hands, their fingers were intertwined as if sharing strength. Sharing a bond.

Whenever he saw the piece, Alexei felt a thump in the region of his heart. An awareness of how lucky he was to have Mina. This year had been everything he could have hoped and it made him more determined to keep what he had.

Smiling, he put his hand to his pocket and turned towards the door, only to pull up short.

The woman he adored stood there, wearing a curiously unreadable expression and a stunning dress of flame red. Alexei's lungs expanded on an appreciative breath as he took in the tiny shoulder straps and flirty skirt that were an invitation to explore.

'Mina! You look stunning.' He imagined his hands skimming her taut thighs beneath the fabric. Heat circled his chest and drove straight to his groin.

'You don't look so bad yourself.' She crossed the room and kissed him. Alexei gathered her up, relishing the fire that ignited between them and the sweet sensation of coming home. Coming to Mina.

When he ended the kiss, he kept his arms

around her. Her exotic spice and cinnamon scent was warm in his nostrils and he savoured how right this was.

'I heard from Carissa today.'

'Hmm?' He looked down into velvety eyes. She was smiling.

'She and Pierre are visiting Ralph in Jeirut. He's thriving and even picking up some of the language.'

Belatedly Alexei caught the thread of the conversation. Ralph Carter. In Jeirut.

Mina walked her fingers up Alexei's chest, making him wish she'd found him naked in the shower.

'It was a stroke of genius, getting him involved in your programme there.'

Alexei shook his head. 'It was as much your idea as mine. You suggested Jeirut.' Because the opportunities for gambling there were limited, so Ralph would have less temptation.

Alexei had revised his view of Ralph when he learned of his gambling addiction, a coping mechanism to deal with overwhelming grief at his wife's death.

After hearing of the older man's shame and desperate plan to pay back the money by gambling more, and his near suicidal despair when that failed, Alexei hadn't pressed charges. Prison wouldn't get his money back. Instead he'd co-opted Ralph into the initiative he and Sheikh Huseyn had begun to give unemployed youth the skills and confidence to start up innovative businesses.

After a rocky start, Ralph, with his financial expertise, pernickety attention to detail and genuine interest in his budding entrepreneurs, was a surprise hit. It helped them and gave him back a sense of purpose and self-respect.

'But you were the one who suggested including him.' Mina's fingers reached his chin and traced his jaw, teasing. 'You gave him a second chance. Not many people would do that.' The way she looked at him stirred Alexei's soul. His chest swelled.

'Everyone deserves a second chance, sweetheart.'

She smiled and Alexei felt the radiance of it all the way to the centre of his being. 'Which shows how right I was about you, Alexei Katsaros. You might be savvy and übersuccessful, but there's more to you than business.'

'Oh, much more.' He slid his hands down Mina's back, over that pertly rounded rump, and pulled her against him. That was better. Much better.

Mina wriggled and Alexei was tempted to forget their plans to attend a new exhibition. Except he had other plans too. A romantic dinner for two in one of the city's best restaurants as a prelude to something much more significant.

But looking into Mina's smiling face, Alexei knew it wasn't a picture-perfect setting that mattered. It was her. And how she felt. Suddenly he couldn't wait.

'Mina.' He swallowed, trying to eradicate the betraying husky edge to his voice. 'I have something for you.'

She blinked. 'That's a coincidence. I have something for you too. Over there—'

'Sweetheart.' Alexei turned her head back towards him and reached into his pocket. 'I've waited a whole year to give you time to be sure of me and what you feel. I'm in love with you, Mina. I want to spend my life with you.'

He'd spent hours thinking of how to say this, searching for something unique and memorable. But when he looked into Mina's warm gaze, each carefully crafted word disintegrated and he was left with the bare truth. 'Will you marry me?'

He lifted his hand and showed her the ring

he'd had made for her. A unique, modern piece of white gold and a square-cut ruby. Sparks shot off the facets as it trembled in the light.

Mina's hand closed around his and he realised they were both shaking. He heard a muffled gasp and saw her eyes were overbright.

'Mina? Sweetheart?'

She shook her head and smiled, her mouth a crumpled curve. 'That sounds like a wonderful plan. I love you too, darling. And yes, I want to be with you, always.'

Elation surged so high he felt ten feet tall. Alexei bent to kiss her but her fingertips on his lips stopped him. 'You don't want to see my gift?'

'Sorry?'

'My gift.' Mina reached over to a nearby table and picked up a small box. She flipped the lid and there were two matching wedding rings. 'I thought a year was time enough. I want you with all my heart, Alexei.' She laughed, the sound like liquid crystal, shining with promise. 'It seems we both had the same idea.'

'Because we're perfectly matched.' He spared an appreciative glance for the finely crafted wedding bands, then lifted her hand and slid the engagement ring onto her finger. Emotion threatened to overwhelm him.

'We definitely are.' She moved her fingers, admiring the ring. 'Thank you, Alexei. I never thought I could be so happy.'

'Nor did I.' He raised her hand to his lips and kissed it. 'And this is just the beginning.' Then he scooped her up and swung her round till the room rang with her delicious laughter. It was a sound he looked forward to hearing for the rest of his life.

* * * * *